CHRISTMAS CAROL MURDER

Books by Leslie Meier

MISTLETOE MURDER

TIPPY TOE MURDER

TRICK OR TREAT MURDER

BACK TO SCHOOL MURDER

VALENTINE MURDER

CHRISTMAS COOKIE MURDER

TURKEY DAY MURDER

WEDDING DAY MURDER

BIRTHDAY PARTY MURDER

FATHER'S DAY MURDER

STAR SPANGLED MURDER

NEW YEAR'S EVE MURDER

BAKE SALE MURDER

CANDY CANE MURDER

ST. PATRICK'S DAY MURDER

MOTHER'S DAY MURDER

WICKED WITCH MURDER

GINGERBREAD COOKIE MURDER

ENGLISH TEA MURDER

CHOCOLATE COVERED MURDER

EASTER BUNNY MURDER

CHRISTMAS CAROL MURDER

Published by Kensington Publishing Corporation

A Lucy Stone Mystery

CHRISTMAS CAROL MURDER

LESLIE MEIER

KENSINGTON BOOKS
www.kensingtonbooks.com

KENSINGTON BOOKS are published by

Kensington Publishing Corp.
119 West 40th Street
New York, NY 10018

All Kensington titles, imprints, and distributed lines are available at special quantity discounts for bulk purchases for sales promotion, premiums, fund-raising, educational, or institutional use.

Special book excerpts or customized printings can also be created to fit specific needs. For details, write or phone the office of the Kensington Special Sales Manager: Attn. Special Sales Department. Kensington Publishing Corp., 119 West 40th Street, New York, NY 10018. Phone: 1-800-221-2647.

Kensington and the K logo Reg. U.S. Pat. & TM Off.

Library of Congress Card Catalogue Number: 2013940650

ISBN-13: 978-0-7582-7701-5
ISBN-10: 0-7582-7701-6
First Kensington Hardcover Edition: October 2013

eISBN-13: 978-0-7582-7703-9
eISBN-10: 0-7582-7703-2
First Kensington Electronic Edition: October 2013

10 9 8 7 6 5 4 3 2

Printed in the United States of America

CHRISTMAS CAROL MURDER

Prologue

IVCET
That was easy, thought Jake Marlowe, cackling merrily as he wrote EVICT in the blanks of the word jumble with a small stub of pencil—waste not, want not was his favorite saying, and he was certainly not going to discard a perfectly usable pencil, even if it was a bit hard to grip with his arthritic hands—and applied himself to the riddle: "Santa's favorite meal." Then, doubting his choice, he wondered if the correct answer was really CIVET. But no, then the *I* and *C* wouldn't be in the squares with circles inside indicating the letters needed to solve the riddle, and he needed them for MILK AND COOKIES, which was undoubtedly the correct answer.

He tossed the paper and pencil on the kitchen table, where the dirty breakfast dishes vied for space with a month's worth of morning papers and junk mail and, pressing his hands on the table for support, rose to his feet. He pushed his wire-rimmed glasses back up his beaky nose and adjusted the belt on his black and brown striped terry cloth bathrobe, lifting the collar against the chill. The antique kerosene heater he used rather than the central heating, which guzzled expensive oil, didn't provide much heat. He picked up his empty coffee mug and shuffled over to the counter where the drip coffeepot sat surrounded by old coffee cans, empty milk containers, and assorted bottles. He filled his stained, chipped mug with the *Downeast Mortgage Company* logo and carried it back to the table, sitting down heavily in his captain's chair, and preparing to settle in with the *Wall Street Journal*.

INTEREST RATES HIT RECORD LOW read the headline, causing him to scowl in disapproval. What were the feds thinking? The economy would never recover at this rate, not if investors couldn't reap some positive gains. He snorted and gulped some coffee. What could you expect? People didn't save anymore; they spent more than they had and then they borrowed to make up the difference, and when they got in trouble, which was inevitable, they expected the government to bail them out. He folded the paper with a snap and added it to the stack beside his chair, a stack that was in danger of toppling over.

Jake had saved every issue of the *Portland Press Herald* that he'd ever received, as well as his copies of the *Wall Street Journal*, and since he was well into his sixties that was quite a lot of papers. They covered every surface in his house, were stacked on windowsills and piled on the floor, filling most of the available space and leaving only narrow pathways that wound from room to room.

Jake never threw anything away. He literally had every single item he'd ever owned stashed somewhere in the big old Victorian house. Pantry shelves were filled with empty jelly jars, kitchen drawers were packed to bursting with plastic bags, closets in the numerous bedrooms were stuffed with old clothes and dozens of pairs of old shoes, the leather cracked and the toes curling up. Beds no one ever slept in were covered with boxes of junk, dresser drawers that were never opened contained old advertising flyers, dead batteries, and blown lightbulbs. And everywhere, filling every bit of square footage, were stacks of newspapers. They crawled up the walls, they blocked windows, they turned the house into a maze of narrow, twisting corridors.

When the grandfather clock in the hall chimed nine, time for Jake to get dressed, he shuffled into the next room, once the dining room but now his bedroom, where he slept on an ancient daybed. He sat down heavily, amid the musty sheets and blankets, and began carefully removing the plastic laundry bag from his heavily starched shirt. He was folding up the plastic bag, intending to add it to the sizeable collection he was accumulating beneath his bed, when he heard the neighbor's dog bark.

It was the mail, right on time; he nodded with satisfaction. Jake was one of the first on Wilf Lundgren's route, and the mail was always delivered around nine, barring the occasional storm delay. Fred, the elderly beagle belonging to his neighbor and dentist, Dr. Cyrus Frost, always announced Wilf's arrival, as well as that of the FedEx truck, the garbage truck, and any proselytizing Jehovah's Witnesses.

Jake was expecting his bank statement, which had been delayed a day because of the Thanksgiving holiday, so he decided to collect the mail even though he wasn't dressed. Not that it mattered. He was decent, covered chin to ankles in the long johns he wore all winter; the thick robe was warm and he had fleece-lined slippers. He hurried down the drive, eager to see if the bank statement had come, and as he approached the mailbox he noticed something large and colorful sticking out of it.

Reaching the box, which topped a post next to the street, he examined a padded mailing envelope printed with a red and green Christmas design protruding from the box. A present? He pulled it out, studying the design of candy canes and gingerbread men. It was addressed to him, he saw, and there was a label that warned *Do Not Open Till Christmas*. It was only the day after Thanksgiving, a bit early for a Christmas gift, perhaps, but Thanksgiving was the official beginning of the Christmas season. Not that he had partaken of the annual feast the day before; he and his partner Ben Scribner had gone to the office as usual, but they had agreed to give their secretary, Elsie Morehouse, the day off. They hadn't wanted to, but Elsie had pointed out in no uncertain terms that it was a legal holiday and she was entitled to take it.

Jake pulled the rest of his mail, a couple of plain white envelopes, out of the box. He noted with satisfaction that the bank statement had finally arrived, and looked forward to balancing it. He took pride in the fact that should there be a discrepancy between his calculations and those of the bank, his would undoubtedly be correct and the error would be the bank's. But first things first. He hurried back to the house, hugging the package to his chest, chuckling merrily.

A present. He hadn't received a present in a long time. Who could it be from? He studied the return address, but it didn't make any sense. *Santa Claus,* it read. *North Pole, Alaska.* It must be some sort of joke. Ben Scribner wasn't known for jokes, so he doubted it was from him. Besides, despite their long partnership of over thirty years, they never exchanged presents.

Perhaps it was from a grateful customer, a home owner who had the good sense to appreciate the current low interest rates, sometimes under four percent. That was unlikely, however, thought Jake. Real estate wasn't what it once was—prices were falling and most home owners owed more than their houses were worth.

The economy was bad, no doubt about it. Maybe some tradesman was expressing appreciation for his custom. He did have a faucet replaced this year; maybe it was a thank you from Earle Plumbing. Ed Earle was probably thankful for one customer who paid on time, cash on the barrelhead. Come to think of it, he'd hired the electrician, too, to fix a busted wall switch. Al Lucier was no doubt appreciative of his prompt payment. Or maybe it was from his insurance agent, who might be sending something more substantial than the usual calendar this year. Only one way to find out, he decided, clutching the package to his chest and hurrying out of the cold and back into the slightly warmer house.

Once inside, with the kitchen door closed behind him, he set the envelopes on the kitchen counter, on top of a stack of empty egg cartons, and carefully examined the package. Only one way to find out what was inside, he decided, and that was to open it. Practically bursting with anticipation, he ripped off the flap.

Chapter One

When the first foreclosure sale of the Great Recession took place in Tinker's Cove, Maine, *Pennysaver* reporter Lucy Stone expected a scene right out of a silent movie. The auctioneer would be a slimy sort of fellow who ran his fingers along his waxed and curled mustache and cackled evilly, the banker would be a chubby chap whose pocket watch dangled from a thick gold chain stretched across his round stomach, and a burly sheriff would be forcibly evicting a noticeably hungry and poorly clad family from their home while his deputies tossed furniture and personal belongings onto the lawn.

The reality, which she discovered when she joined a small group of people gathered in front of a modest three-bedroom ranch, was somewhat different. For one thing, the house was vacant. The home owners had left weeks ago, according to a neighbor. "When Jim lost his job at the car dealership they realized they couldn't keep up the payments on Patty's income—she was a home health aide—so they packed up their stuff and left. Patty's mom has a B and B on Cape Cod, so she's going to help out there, and Jim's got himself enrolled in a nursing program at a community college."

"That sounds like a good plan," Lucy said, feeling rather disappointed as she'd hoped to write an emotion-packed human interest story.

"They're not getting off scot-free," the neighbor said, a young mother with a toddler on her hip. "They'll lose all the money they put in the house—bamboo floors, granite countertops, not to mention all the payments they made—and the foreclosure will be a blot on their credit rating for years. . . ." Her voice trailed off as the auctioneer called for attention and began reading a lot of legalese.

While he spoke, Lucy studied the individuals in the small group, who she assumed were planning to bid on the property in hopes of snagging a bargain. One or two were even holding white envelopes, most likely containing certified checks for the ten thousand dollars down specified in the ad announcing the sale.

But when the auctioneer called for bids, Ben Scribner, a partner in Downeast Mortgage, which held the note, opened with $185,000, the principal amount. That was more than the bargain hunters were prepared to offer, and they began to leave. Seeing no further offers, the auctioneer declared the sale over and the property now owned by the mortgage company.

Ben, who had thick white hair and ruddy cheeks, was dressed in the casual outfit of khaki pants and button-down oxford shirt topped by a barn coat favored by businessmen in the coastal Maine town. He was a prominent citizen who spoke out at town meetings, generally against any measure that would raise taxes. His company, Downeast Mortgage, provided financing for

CHRISTMAS CAROL MURDER   9

much of the region and there were few people in town who hadn't done business with him and his partner, Jake Marlowe. Marlowe was well known as a cheapskate, living like a solitary razor clam in that ramshackle Victorian mansion, and he was a fixture on the town's Finance Committee where he kept an eagle eye on the town budget.

Since that October day three years ago, there had been many more foreclosures in Tinker's Cove as the economy ground to a standstill. People moved in with relatives, they rented, or they moved on. What they didn't do was launch any sort of protest, at least not until now.

The fax announcing a Black Friday demonstration had come into the *Pennysaver* from a group at Winchester College calling itself the Social Action Committee, or SAC, which claimed to represent "the ninety-nine percent." The group was calling for an immediate end to foreclosures and was planning a demonstration at the Downeast Mortgage office on the Friday after Thanksgiving, which Lucy had been assigned to cover.

When she arrived, a few minutes before the appointed time of nine a.m., there was no sign of any demonstration. But when the clock on the Community Church chimed the hour, a row of marchers suddenly issued from the municipal parking lot situated behind the stores that lined Main Street. They were mostly college students who for one reason or other hadn't gone home for the holiday, as well as a few older people, professors and local residents Lucy recognized. They were bundled up against the November chill in colorful ski jackets, and they were carrying signs and marching to the beat of a Bruce Springsteen song issuing from a boom box.

The leader, wearing a camo jacket and waving a mega-phone, was a twenty-something guy with a shaved head.

"What do we want?" he yelled, his voice amplified and filling the street.

"Justice!" the crowd yelled back.

"When do we want it?" he cried.

"NOW!" roared the crowd.

Lucy immediately began snapping photos with her camera, and jogged along beside the group. When they stopped in front of Downeast Mortgage, and the leader got up on a milk crate to speak, she pulled out her note-book. "Who is that guy?" she asked the kid next to her.

"Seth Lesinski," the girl replied.

"Do you know how he spells it?"

"I think it's L-E-S-I-N-S-K-I."

"Got it," Lucy said, raising her eyes and noticing a girl who looked an awful lot like her daughter Sara. With blue eyes, blond hair, and a blue crocheted hat she'd seen her pull on that very morning, it was defi-nitely Sara.

"What are you doing here?" she demanded, con-fronting her college freshman daughter. "I thought you have a poli sci class now."

Sara rolled her eyes. "Mo-om," she growled. "Later, okay?"

"No. You're supposed to be in class. Do you know how much that class costs? I figured it out. It's over a hundred dollars per hour and you're wasting it."

"Well, if you're so concerned about waste, why aren't you worried about all the people losing their homes?" Sara countered. "Huh?"

"I am concerned," Lucy said.

"Well, you haven't shown it. There hasn't been a

word in the paper except for those legal ads announcing the sales."

Lucy realized her daughter had a point. "Well, I'm covering it now," she said.

"So why don't you be quiet and listen to Seth," Sara suggested, causing Lucy's eyes to widen in shock. Sara had never spoken to her like that before, and she was definitely going to have a talk with her. But now, she realized, she was missing Seth's speech.

"Downeast Mortgage is the primary lender in the county and they have foreclosed on dozens of properties, and more foreclosures are scheduled. . . ."

The crowd booed, until Seth held up his hand for silence.

"They'll have you believe that people who miss their payments are deadbeats, failures, lazy, undeserving, irresponsible. . . . You've heard it all, right?"

There was general agreement, and people nodded.

"But the truth is different. These borrowers qualified for mortgages, had jobs that provided enough income to cover the payments, but then the recession came and the jobs were gone. Unemployment in this county is over fourteen percent. That's why people are losing their homes."

Lucy knew there was an element of truth in what Lesinski was saying. She knew that even the town government, until recently the region's most dependable employer, had recently laid off a number of employees and cut the hours of several others. In fact, scanning the crowd, she recognized Lexie Cunningham, who was a clerk in the tax collector's office. A big guy in a plaid jacket and navy blue watch cap was standing beside her, probably her husband. Lucy decided they might be good interview subjects and approached them.

"Hi, Lucy," Lexie said, with a little smile. She looked as if she'd lost weight, thought Lucy, and her hair, which had been dyed blond, was now showing dark roots and was pulled back unattractively into a ponytail. "This is my husband, Zach."

"I'm writing this up for the paper," Lucy began. "Can you tell me why you're here today?"

"'Cause we're gonna lose our house, that's why," Zach growled. "Downeast sent us a notice last week."

"My hours were cut, you know," Lexie said. "Now I don't work enough hours to get the health insurance benefit. Because of that we have to pay the entire premium—it's almost two thousand dollars a month, which is actually more than I now make. We can't pay both the mortgage and the health insurance and we can't drop the health insurance because of Angie—she's got juvenile kidney disease."

"I didn't know," Lucy said, realizing they were faced with an impossible choice.

"We don't qualify for assistance. Zach makes too much and we're over the income limit by a couple hundred dollars. But the health insurance is expensive, more than our mortgage. We were just getting by but then Angie had a crisis and the bills started coming. . . ."

"But you do have health insurance," Lucy said.

"It doesn't cover everything. There are copays and coinsurance and exclusions. . . ."

"Downeast is a local company—have you talked to Marlowe and Scribner? I bet they'd understand. . . ."

Zach started laughing, revealing a missing rear molar. "Understand? All those guys understand is that I agreed to pay them nine hundred and forty-five dollars every month. That's my problem, is what they told me."

"So that's why we're out here, demonstrating," Lexie said, as a sudden huge boom shook the ground under their feet.

"What the . . . ?" Everyone was suddenly silent, shocked by the loud noise and the reverberations.

"Gas?" somebody asked. They could hear a dog barking.

"Fire," said a kid in a North Face jacket, pointing to the column of black smoke that was rising into the sky.

"Parallel Street," Zach said, as sirens wailed and bright red fire trucks went roaring down the street, lights flashing.

A couple of guys immediately took off down the street, running after the fire trucks, and soon the crowd followed. Lucy always felt a little uncomfortably ghoulish at times like this, but she knew it was simply human nature to want to see what was going on. She knew it was the same impulse that caused people to watch CNN and listen to the car radio and even read the *Pennysaver*.

So she joined the crowd, hurrying along beside Sara and her friend Amy, rounding the corner onto Maple Street, where the smell of burning was stronger, and on to Parallel Street, which, as its name suggested, ran parallel to Main Street. Unlike Main Street, which was the town's commercial center, Parallel was a residential street filled with big old houses set on large properties. Most had been built in the nineteenth century by prosperous sea captains, eager to showcase their success. Nowadays, a few were still single family homes owned by members of the town's professional elite, but others had been subdivided into apartments and B and Bs. It was a pleasant street, lined with trees, and the houses were generally well maintained. In the summer, geraniums bloomed in window boxes and the sound of lawn mowers was frequently heard. Now, some houses still displayed pumpkin and gourd decorations for Thanksgiving while others were trimmed for Christmas, with window boxes filled with evergreen boughs and red-ribboned wreaths hung on the front doors. All except for one house, a huge Victorian owned by Jake Marlowe that was generally considered a blight on the neighborhood.

The old house was a marvel of Victorian design, boasting a three-story tower, numerous chimneys, bay windows, a sunroom, and a wraparound porch. Passing it, observing the graying siding that had long since lost its paint and the sagging porch, Lucy always imagined the house as it had once been. Then, she thought, the mansion would have sported a colorful paint job and the porch would have been filled with wicker furniture, where long-skirted ladies once sat and sipped lemonade while they observed the passing scene.

It had always seemed odd to her that a man whose business was financing property would take such poor care of his own, but when she'd interviewed a psychiatrist for a feature story about hoarders she began to understand that Jake Marlowe's cheapness was a sort of pathology. "Hoarders can't let anything go; it makes them unbearably anxious to part with anything," the psychiatrist had explained to her.

Now, standing in front of the burning house, Lucy saw that Jake Marlowe was going to lose everything.

"Wow," she said, turning to Sara and noticing how

her daughter's face was glowing, bathed in rosy light from the fire. Everyone's face was like that, she saw, as they watched the orange flames leaping from the windows, running across the tired old porch, and even erupting from the top of the tower. No one could survive such a fire, she thought. It was fortunate it started in the morning, when she assumed Marlowe would be at his Main Street office.

"Back, everybody back," the firemen were saying, pushing the crowd to the opposite side of the street.

They were making no attempt to stop the fire but instead were pouring water on the roofs of neighboring houses, fearing that sparks from the fire would set them alight. More sirens were heard and Lucy realized the call had gone out to neighboring towns for mutual aid.

"What a shame," Lucy said, to nobody in particular, and a few others murmured in agreement.

Not everyone was sympathetic, however. "Serves the mean old bastard right," Zach Cunningham said.

"It's not like he took care of the place," Sara observed.

"He's foreclosed on a lot of people," Lexie Cunningham said. "Now he'll know what it's like to lose his home."

"You said it, man," Seth said, clapping Zach on the shoulder. "What goes around comes around." Realizing the crowd was with him, Seth got up on his milk crate. "Burn, baby, burn!" he yelled, raising his fist.

Lucy was shocked, but the crowd picked up the chant. "Burn, baby, burn!" they yelled back. "Burn, baby, burn."

Disgusted, she tapped Sara on the shoulder, indicating they should leave. Sara, however, shrugged her off and joined the refrain, softly at first but gradually growing louder as she was caught in the excitement of the moment.

Lucy wanted to leave and she wanted Sara to leave, too, but the girl stubbornly ignored her urgings. Finally, realizing she was alone in her sentiments, she shouldered her way through the crowd and headed back to Main Street and the *Pennysaver* office. At the corner, she remembered her job and paused to take a few more pictures for the paper. This would be a front page story, no doubt about it. She was peering through the camera's viewfinder when the tower fell in a shower of sparks and the crowd gave throat to a celebratory cheer.

You would have thought the football team scored a touchdown, she thought, stomping along the sidewalk that tilted this way and that from frost heaves. Nobody cared that a precious bit of the town's heritage was going up in smoke. Nobody but her.

The *Pennysaver* office was empty when she arrived. Phyllis, the receptionist, and Ted, who was publisher, editor, and chief reporter, were most likely at the fire. Good, she thought, he could write the story. She took off her parka and hung it on the coatrack, filled the coffeepot and got it brewing, and then she booted up her computer. She was checking her e-mails when the little bell on the door jangled and Ted entered.

"What are you doing here?" he asked, unwrapping his scarf. "Don't you know Jake Marlowe's house is burning down?" He had removed his Bruins ski cap and was running his fingers through his short, salt and pepper hair.

"I was there. I left."

"How come?" His face was squarish and clean-shaven,

his brow furrowed in concern. "That's not like you, leaving a big story."

"The crowd freaked me out," she said, wrapping her arms across her chest and hugging herself. "Sara was there—she was part of it, screaming along with the rest."

"You know what they say about a mob. It's only as smart as the dumbest member," Ted said, pouring himself a mug of coffee. "Want a cup?"

"Sure," Lucy replied. When he gave her the mug she wrapped her fingers around it for warmth. "I always liked that old house," she said, taking a sip. "I sometimes imagined it the way it used to be. A painted lady, that's what they call those fancy Victorians."

"Marlowe didn't take care of it. It was a firetrap. Truth be told, it should've been condemned and it would've been if Marlowe wasn't such a big shot in town. But he was on the Finance Committee and the fire chief wasn't about to mess with him, not with Marlowe constantly pushing the committee to cut the department's budget."

"I wonder where Marlowe was," Lucy mused, setting her cup down. "I didn't see him in the crowd. Did you?"

Ted tossed the wooden stirrer into the trash and carried his mug over to his desk, an old rolltop he'd inherited from his grandfather, who was a legendary New England newspaperman. "Nope, he wasn't there."

"Maybe he went away for the holiday," Lucy speculated. "Probably for the best. It would be awful to watch your house burn down."

"Yeah," Ted said, clicking away on his keyboard. "I've got a meeting this afternoon over in Gilead. Do me a favor and follow up with the fire chief before you go home."

Lunch was long past and Ted had gone to his meeting when Lucy noticed the rattling of the old wooden Venetian blinds that covered the plate glass windows, indicating the fire trucks were finally returning to the station down the street. A few minutes later Phyllis came in, wearing a faux leopard skin coat and sporting a streak of soot on her face. "Jake Marlowe's house burned to the ground!" she exclaimed. "What a show. Too bad you missed it."

"I was there for a while," Lucy said. "Your face is dirty."

"Oh, thanks." Phyllis hung up her coat and went into the tiny bathroom, lifting the harlequin reading glasses that hung from a chain around her neck as she went. "Look at that," Lucy heard her saying. "It's soot from the fire. And no wonder—that old house is still smoldering."

"It was some blaze," Lucy said.

Phyllis sat at her desk and applied a liberal glob of hand lotion. "I wonder how it started," she said.

"There was an explosion," Lucy said, suddenly remembering the boom that had disrupted the SAC demonstration.

"Must've been gas—I don't know why people mess around with that stuff. It's awfully dangerous."

"I wonder," Lucy said, reaching for the phone and dialing. In a moment of madness, when he was looking for publicity for a food drive, Chief Buzz Bresnahan had given her his personal cell phone number. Lucy was careful not to abuse the privilege, but today she figured his secretary would be blocking calls.

"Lucy," he barked. "Make it fast."

"Okay. Any idea how the fire started? Was it a gas leak?"

"Not gas. We're not sure. The fire marshal is investigating. It's definitely suspicious."

"Any injuries?"

"No, I'm happy to say," Bresnahan replied. "Gotta go. You better check with the fire marshal's office. I'm pretty sure this is going to turn out to be a case of arson."

"Arson?" Lucy asked, but Buzz had already gone.

Chapter Two

Several firemen and a police patrol remained at the site of the fire through the weekend, watching for flare-ups and keeping thrill seekers and souvenir hunters away from the smoldering pile of rubble. On Monday the fire marshal's team arrived, along with two trained dogs, Blaze and Spark. It didn't take Blaze very long to make a disturbing discovery: the ruins contained a badly burned body, most probably that of the owner, Jake Marlowe.

Lucy finally got confirmation from police chief Jim Kirwan on Wednesday, just before deadline. "Yup, Lucy," he said, "it was definitely murder. Somebody sent Marlowe a mail bomb. It blew up in his face when he opened it."

"Are they sure it was actually Marlowe?" Lucy asked. "I thought there wasn't much left."

"It was definitely Marlowe. His body was in the kitchen. Well, where the kitchen used to be. And Dr. Frost, the dentist who lives next door, recognized some bridgework he did for Marlowe."

"How can they tell it was a mail bomb?" Lucy asked. "Didn't the fire destroy the evidence?"

"I don't know the details; all I know is what the state fire marshal tells me and he says it was a mail bomb. No doubt about it."

"Was it mailed locally?"

"Uh, that he didn't know," Kirwan admitted. "We've got the post office working on it, but the assumption is that it was a local job. Think about it: Marlowe wasn't very popular around town. A lot of people have lost, or are about to lose, their homes to Downeast Mortgage. And Marlowe didn't do himself any favors with that Fin-Com vote cutting town employees' hours. No, we've got suspects coming out of the woodwork, lots of them." He chuckled. "Which reminds me, Lucy. Who's holding your mortgage?"

Lucy found herself grinning. "Nobody. We paid ours off last year."

"Lucky devils," Jim said. "I wish I hadn't refinanced back in two thousand seven when all the so-called financial experts were saying it was the thing to do. Now I'm underwater, like most everybody else in town. I owe more than the house is worth."

"Just hang on," Lucy advised. "Prices will go back up; they always do."

"I dunno," Kirwan said. "This is one time I kinda feel for the guy who did it. Truth is, I would've liked to do it myself."

"I'm assuming that's off the record," Lucy said.

"Uh, yeah," Kirwan said.

Sitting in Jake's Donut Shop on Thursday morning—this long-time Tinker's Cove institution was named after its owner, Jake Prose—Lucy was staring at the front page photo of Marlowe's burning mansion and mourning the quote she couldn't use. What a bombshell that would have been! Police chief goes rogue! If only she hadn't promised to keep his revealing statement off the record.

"Hey, Lucy." It was her best friend, Sue Finch, and Lucy hopped up to greet her with a hug.

"Some fire," Sue said, glancing at the paper as she took her seat and shrugged out of her shearling coat.

Lucy tapped the head of a small figure standing in the crowd. "That's Sara. She was supposed to be in class but she was out demonstrating with the college's Social Action Committee."

"So Sara's suddenly developed a social conscience?" Sue asked, removing her beret and smoothing her glossy black pageboy with her beautifully manicured hands. "I'm only asking because that leader, Seth, is pretty good looking." She was pointing to the photo of Seth, his fist raised in defiance.

"You think she's interested in him, not the issues?" Lucy asked. She hadn't considered this possibility.

Sue rolled her eyes. "Yes, I do. And by the way, what do I have to do to get a cup of coffee around here?"

Norine, the waitress, was on it. "Sorry, Sue. I got distracted," she said, setting a couple of mugs on the table and filling them. "Ever since the fire I just can't seem to concentrate." She shuddered. "I didn't like Marlowe—nobody did—but that's a terrible way to go."

"You said it," Pam Stillings chimed in, arriving with Rachel Goodman. Pam was married to Lucy's boss, Ted, and she and Rachel completed the group of four friends who met for breakfast every Thursday at Jake's.

"That poor man," Rachel added, lowering her big doe eyes and shaking her head. Rachel was a soft touch, who provided home care for the town's oldest resident, Miss Julia Ward Howe Tilley.

"He wasn't poor," Lucy said, knowing perfectly well that Rachel hadn't been referring to Marlowe's finances. "He was making a bundle off those mortgages and almost everybody in town has one. Chief Kirwan told me he's got more suspects than he can count."

Norine arrived with coffee for Rachel and green tea for Pam, who ate only natural, organic foods. "You girls want the usual?" she asked. Receiving nods all round, she departed, writing on her order pad as she went.

"Let's not talk about the fire," Rachel suggested. "I've got big news."

"Go on," Sue urged. She didn't like dramatic pauses unless she was making them.

"I'm directing the Community Players' holiday production," Rachel announced. "It's Dickens's *A Christmas Carol,* and I want you all to audition."

"Count me out," Sue said, shaking her head. "I couldn't act my way out of a paper bag but I'll be happy to handle the refreshments."

"Great," Rachel said. "But I think you'd make a fabulous Ghost of Christmas Past."

"That's a joke, right?" Sue asked suspiciously.

"Yeah," Rachel admitted. "But I do think Lucy would be great as Mrs. Cratchit. She's so warm and motherly."

"Me?" Lucy didn't recognize herself in that description.

"Actually, yes," Sue said. "You are warm and motherly, even grandmotherly."

Lucy gave her friend a dirty look. "I adore Patrick,"

she said, naming her son Toby's little boy, "but you have to admit I'm a young grandmother."

"My grandmother wore thick stockings and lace-up oxfords with heels," Pam recalled. "White in the summer and black after Labor Day. I don't think they make them anymore. Her breasts went down to her waist and she wore her gray hair in a bun."

"Fortunately for Lucy they've invented underwire bras and hair dye," Sue remarked.

"And sneakers," Lucy added, naming her favorite footwear as Norine delivered her order of two eggs over easy with corned beef hash and whole wheat toast. Norine passed Rachel her usual Sunshine muffin, gave Pam her yogurt topped with granola, and refilled Sue's cup with coffee.

"Auditions are tonight," Rachel said. "Will you come, Lucy? And how about you, Pam?"

"Ofay," Lucy agreed, her mouth full of buttery toast.

"I'm too busy for rehearsals," Pam said, "but I can do the program for you. I'll get ads and Ted can design it and get it printed."

"That would be great," Rachel said. "Any money we make will go to the Hat and Mitten Fund."

They all nodded in approval. The Hat and Mitten Fund, which provided warm clothing and school supplies for the town's needy children, was a favorite charity.

"Maybe we could give part of the money to the Cunninghams," Lucy suggested. "They're having a hard time right now. Their little girl, Angie, has kidney disease and there are a lot of expenses their health insurance doesn't cover."

"That's a good idea, Lucy," Pam said, a member of

the town Finance Committee. "Lexie is one of the town employees whose hours were cut."

"How awful for them," Rachel said. "Just having a sick child is bad enough, but now the Cunninghams have all these financial worries, too."

"They may lose their house," Lucy said.

"Oh," Pam groaned. "I feel so responsible."

"But you voted against those cuts," Sue said.

"The vote was three to two," Pam said. "Frankie and I were the nays—we were outnumbered by the men." She paused. "But now that Marlowe is no longer with us there's a vacancy on the board. Right now we're evenly divided. Taubert and Hawthorne have one goal: keep taxes low. Frankie and I aren't exactly big spenders, but we have a more moderate approach. We need to fill that vacancy with another moderate who understands the value of town services."

"And town employees," Rachel added.

"You're right," Pam said. "Marlowe actually called them parasites who were sucking the taxpayers dry."

"Sounds like a real sweetheart," Sue said sarcastically.

"Not really," Pam said. "So if you can think of anybody who'd be willing to take on a thoroughly thankless task by joining the FinCom, let me know. We want to choose someone at the next meeting."

"Ted did put an announcement in the paper," Lucy said. "Maybe you'll get some volunteers."

"It's a bad time of year to recruit a new member," Pam said. "Everybody's busy with Christmas."

"That's true," Lucy said, remembering that her husband, Bill, had recently expressed a desire to become more active in town affairs. Maybe this was something he'd be interested in doing. She filed that thought for later and turned her attention to her friends.

"Don't forget the auditions tonight," Rachel was saying. "At the Community Church. Can I count on you, Lucy?"

"Okay," Lucy agreed. The audition would make a nice human interest story and she was certain there was no way she was going to get a role. She was no Mrs. Cratchit, for sure.

After leaving Jake's, Lucy spent a few hours at the *Pennysaver*, filing news releases and typing up events for the Things to Do This Week column. As Phyllis had pointed out, there were more listings than usual, because of Christmas. All of the churches were holding bazaars, the Historical Society was having a cookie sale, and the high school was giving a holiday concert. Going beyond Tinker's Cove, the Gilead Artists were having a small works sale, the South Coast Horticultural Society was holding a gala Festival of Trees and the Coastal Chorale invited one and all to join them in singing Handel's *Messiah*.

"If you did all these things you wouldn't have any time to shop or wrap presents or send Christmas cards," Lucy observed.

"Nobody sends Christmas cards anymore," said Phyllis, who ought to know because her husband, Wilf, was a mail carrier. "They e-mail holiday greetings."

"I never thought of that," Lucy said.

"Well, don't," Phyllis said. "The postal service is having enough problems. They need the business."

"They can count on me," Lucy said. "I always send cards and I like getting them. I put them up around the kitchen door."

She was typing the listing for the preschool story hour when she had an unsettling thought. "Phyllis, did Wilf deliver that postal bomb they think killed Jake Marlowe?"

Phyllis wrapped her fuzzy purple sweater tightly across her ample bosom and blinked behind her pink and black harlequin reading glasses. "I think he must have," she said in a very small voice. "I know the state police have questioned him."

"They don't think . . ." Lucy began.

"I certainly hope not!" Phyllis exclaimed. "He was just doing his job, delivering the mail. He doesn't know what's in the packages—how could he?"

"Of course not," Lucy said. But she was thinking how terrible it would have been if the bomb had exploded early. And seeing Phyllis's bleak expression, Lucy knew her coworker was thinking the very same thing.

When Lucy left the office she checked her list of errands. She needed to cash a check at the bank, the wreaths she'd ordered from the high school cheerleaders were awaiting pickup, and she had to do her weekly grocery shopping. First stop, she decided, was the drive-through at the bank, which was at one end of Main Street. Then she'd zip down Parallel Street to the school, avoiding traffic, and get the wreaths. From there she could sneak into the IGA parking lot from the back, missing the traffic light on Main Street.

She hadn't forgotten about the fire, but she was distracted, making plans for Christmas as she drove along Parallel Street, so it was quite a shock when Marlowe's burned house came into view. She immediately slowed the car, taking in the scorched chimneys, the flame-scarred walls, and the stinking, blackened pile of debris surrounded by a fluttering yellow ribbon of *DO NOT CROSS* tape that was all that remained of the once magnificent house. She'd seen fires before, of course. Fires were big news and she'd had to cover quite a few in her career, but she'd rarely seen one that was so completely destructive. Marlowe's burned-out house was a frightening sight, especially to someone like her, who also happened to live in an antique house.

Batteries, she reminded herself, pressing the accelerator. Don't forget to buy fresh batteries for the smoke alarms.

Not surprisingly, the IGA was out of nine-volt batteries, even the expensive brand-name ones. "We're expecting a shipment on Saturday," said Dot Kirwan, the cashier, who also happened to be police chief Jim Kirwan's mother. Her son Todd was also a police officer, and her daughter, Krissy, the town's emergency dispatcher. Dot was well connected and Lucy cultivated her as a prime source of information. "There's been a run on them since the fire. You're supposed to change the batteries when you put your clock back in the spring but it seems that a lot of folks aren't going to wait. They're doing it while it's fresh on their mind."

"Any progress on the fire?" Lucy asked, as she began to unload her cart.

"Not that I've heard," Dot said. She had permed gray hair cut short and wore a bright red smock with her official IGA name tag pinned on her left breast. "They sent some stuff to the crime lab, but I don't think they're going to learn much more than they already know. It was a mail bomb—anybody could've sent it."

"Anybody who knows how to make a mail bomb," Lucy said.

"There's instructions on the Internet," Dot said. "You could make one, if you wanted."

"Well, I don't," Lucy said.

"Me, either." Dot scanned a package of veggie burgers, a mainstay of Sara's diet. "Tell the truth, I kind of miss old Jake. He was a regular customer, came in most days."

"Really?" Lucy was bagging her groceries in the reusable bags that her daughters Sara and Zoe insisted she use.

"Yup. He kept an eye on the dented cans, the day-old bread, even the marked-down meat. He loved a bargain." She paused. "That comes to a hundred thirty-six dollars and seventy-four cents."

Lucy swiped her debit card and punched her code into the keypad. "I guess I'd be rich, too, if I didn't spend all my money on groceries and gas and clothes. . . ."

"That's the secret," said Ike Stoughton, who was buying coffee, sugar, and creamer for his office. "Jake didn't spend much, that's for sure. Never paid more than he had to. I'll miss him, though."

"You're one of the few," Dot said dryly.

Lucy knew Ike, a neighbor, was a highly regarded surveyor. "Did you do much work for Marlowe?" she asked.

"Not too much lately, but a few years ago he took a lot of land by adverse possession and I did the surveying for him." He paused, then cocked an eyebrow. "He didn't pay much, but he was as good as his word and he did pay on time."

Lucy, whose husband, Bill, was a restoration carpenter, knew that all too often clients held back final payments, demanding work they hadn't contracted for, and sometimes paid late or didn't make that final payment until threatened with a lawsuit. "Old time values," Lucy said. "You don't see them so much anymore."

"These days most people can't afford them," Dot said.

"True," Ike agreed, taking his package and nodding toward the big plate glass window at the front of the store. "Looks like snow," he said, and Lucy saw the sky was filling fast with dark clouds.

Chapter Three

A few snowflakes were floating about when Lucy turned off Red Top Road and into her driveway, but they melted as soon as they hit the ground and there was no accumulation. The house was empty, except for Libby the Lab, who gave her a perfunctory greeting before turning to her main interest, which was sniffing at the grocery bags Lucy had set on the floor. She found the one with the chicken in a matter of seconds and Lucy quickly grabbed it and hoisted it on to the kitchen counter.

"Okay," she told the dog. "I know it's hard, all this food and nothing for you."

Libby sat on her haunches and stared at her with her big brown eyes. "I'll play the game if you insist," she seemed to be saying, "even though we both know I'm the boss around here."

Lucy obediently began digging around in the grocery bags until she found the bag of beef jerky treats and gave a couple to Libby, who wolfed them down. "That's all, now," she said, in a firm tone, and the dog slouched off to settle down on her bed. There she set her chin on her paws and watched with interest as Lucy put the groceries away.

That chore done, she popped a chicken and some sweet potatoes in the oven, then began unloading the dishwasher. From time to time she peeked out the window to check on the snow, but it wasn't amounting to much, so the roads would be okay for her returning family members. Zoe was the first to arrive home; now that her friend Amy Whitmore had a driver's license she got a ride with her most days, shunning the school bus.

Bill was next, in his pickup truck. He was a restoration carpenter and had landed a big contract converting an old meetinghouse in nearby Gilead into a walk-in health clinic. He sniffed the air, decided it was chicken roasting, and gave her a peck on the cheek. "Shall I open that chardonnay?" he asked, and receiving a nod, got to work with a corkscrew.

They had just seated themselves at the round oak kitchen table with their glasses of wine when Sara blew in. "Sorry I'm late," she said, unwinding her scarf, striped in the green and white that were Winchester College's colors. "I forgot the time."

"No problem," Lucy said, sipping her wine. "Dinner won't be ready for another fifteen minutes."

"Great." She thundered up the back stairway and slammed the door to her room shut.

"Funny," Bill said. "I thought girls would be quieter than boys."

"Not that I've noticed," Lucy said, laughing.

Promptly at six, what sounded like a herd of elephants but was only Zoe and Sara came pounding down the stairs, looking for dinner. The girls quickly set the dining room table while Lucy dished up the chicken, baked sweet potatoes, green beans, and salad.

"So what's new?" Bill asked, slicing into the chicken with his carving knife.

"The junior class is having a toy drive for Christmas," Zoe said. "I'm in charge of publicity."

"I can help with that," Lucy offered, serving herself salad. "What about you, Sara? Is the college holding a holiday fund-raiser?"

Sara was helping herself to a baked sweet potato. "Charity at Christmas is just a sop, to make people feel good about themselves. The Social Action Committee is working for real economic justice. When we achieve that, charity will be unnecessary—everyone's needs will be met."

"A lofty goal," Bill said.

"And until then, a lot of people right here in Tinker's Cove are in need," Lucy added.

"And the little kids shouldn't have to suffer," Zoe said. "Not at Christmas."

"Christmas is just a day like any other, that's what Seth says. He says Christmas is just a corporate gimmick to get people to spend money they don't have and to distract them from the real problem, which is an economic system that benefits only one percent of the population while the other ninety-nine percent are struggling."

"Who's Seth?" Bill asked, zeroing in on an unfamiliar male name.

"Seth Lesinski. He's amazing, Dad. He's the leader— Well, there are actually no official leaders. . . . He facilitates SAC."

"What's the difference?"

"Oh, he calls the meetings and presents ideas for action, like the protest we had the other day against Downeast Mortgage."

"Sounds like he's the leader," Bill said, helping himself to seconds.

"No, the whole group has to vote."

"Still . . ." Bill began.

"He's very good looking," Lucy interjected. "At least that's what Sue says."

"SAC is not about looks," Sara said, her cheeks flushed with color. "It's not about appearances. It's what we do that's important."

"You've got to admit he cuts quite a dashing figure," Lucy said. "That scarf he wears, and that camo jacket fits like he had it tailored. . . ."

"Don't be ridiculous, Mom."

"Just an observation," Lucy said. "By the way, I'm auditioning tonight. The Community Players are putting on *A Christmas Carol* and Rachel wants me to be Mrs. Cratchit."

"Sentimental Victorian drivel," Sara sniffed.

"Do you really think you can act?" Zoe asked.

"Where are you going to find the time?" Bill asked. "That's if you get the part."

"Not much chance of that," Sara scoffed.

"Rachel thinks I can do it. She asked me specially to audition."

"She's probably just being nice," Zoe said in a consoling voice. "You don't have any acting experience."

"She's right, Mom," Sara said. "You have to have talent to act. Some people can and some people can't. It's genetics."

"You're going to be too busy, anyway, with Christmas and all." Bill ended the discussion by changing the subject. "What's for dessert?"

When Lucy left the house the girls were busy clearing the table and loading the dishwasher, Libby's nose was buried in her dish, and Bill was watching TV. There was about a half inch of wet snow on the ground and she drove cautiously. She'd never auditioned for anything, so she didn't know what to expect, but she thought she might enjoy acting. She was, she admitted to herself, excited at the prospect of trying something new. Wouldn't it be great if she got the part? That would show those naysayers at home!

When she arrived in the basement meeting room at the Community Church she found a handful of people sitting around a couple of tables that had been pushed together. Rachel was there, of course, and so was Bob, her lawyer husband. She recognized a few other people, including Marge Culpepper, and Florence Gallagher, whom she'd recently interviewed for a feature story about the children's books she'd illustrated.

Rachel greeted her with a smile. "Great, you're here, Lucy. I think we can get started. As you can see, I like to keep things very informal. We've got scripts, so we'll read a little bit, and if you have any experience acting, please tell me. Bob, I think we'll start with you. Can you read Scrooge's lines on page five?"

"Is Bob going to be Scrooge?" Lucy couldn't see it. Bob was the sweetest, nicest man she knew. He had a reputation as a bit of a bleeding heart and much of his busy law practice was pro bono.

"Bah! Humbug!" he growled in a very convincing way, and they all laughed.

After he'd read a few lines, complaining to Bob Cratchit about giving him a day off to celebrate Christmas with his family, Rachel thanked him and turned to Lucy.

"Lucy, do you have any acting experience?"

"I do," Lucy said, dredging her memory and coming up with a nugget. "In kindergarten I was Ferdinand the Bull's mother. As I recall, I had a line about how Ferdinand liked to sit quietly and smell the flowers."

"Practically a professional," Rachel said, when the laughter subsided. "I want you to draw on that experience and read Mrs. Cratchit's lines on page thirty-five."

When Lucy finished, Rachel nodded. "Very nice. I think you'll be great."

"You mean I got the part?"

"Absolutely," Rachel said.

After an hour or so Rachel called a break and Lucy struck up a conversation with Marge, who was married to the town's community affairs officer, Barney Culpepper. Marge was going to play the role of Scrooge's housekeeper.

"I wish I'd gotten a more sympathetic role," she said, pouring herself a cup of decaf at the refreshment table. "She pawns his stuff before Scrooge is even buried."

"It's just a foreshadowing, right? It doesn't actually happen," Lucy said. "Just like Tiny Tim doesn't die."

"Oh, now you've wrecked the ending for me," Marge teased.

"Talking about endings, have they made any progress on the fire investigation?"

"Quite a bit of overtime, which comes in handy this time of year. The problem is there are too many suspects. Practically anybody who has a mortgage from

Downeast has a motive and that's most everybody in town."

"Not everybody knows how to make a bomb, though," Lucy said.

"There are instructions on the Internet," Marge said, choosing a chocolate frosted donut. "And a lot of folks in town are very handy, used to making do."

"That's true," Lucy said.

Rachel called them back to work, and when they'd all gathered again at the table she made an announcement. "I'm very happy to say that I think we've filled all the parts, and I'm confident we're going to have a terrific show. Some of you are veterans with the Community Players, so you know the drill. Each actor is expected to raise a hundred dollars by selling ads in our program to finance the production."

"You mean we have to pay to play?" Florence asked, raising one beautifully shaped eyebrow. Lucy knew she must be well into her forties, but thanks to moisturizer, hair color, and visits to the gym, she looked much younger.

"That's one I haven't heard before," Rachel said, "but that's about it." She paused. "Is this going to be a problem for anyone?"

"Can we help some other way?" Florence asked. "I could help with the scenery, for example. I hate to ask people for money."

Rachel sighed. "I know things are tight for everyone right now, and I don't want anyone to leave the show because they can't sell a few ads. Let's just leave it that I expect everyone to do their best to come up with the suggested amount." Receiving nods from the cast members, she moved on. "Okay, let's do a read-through and take it from the top."

Friday morning Lucy was crowing about getting the part of Mrs. Cratchit, despite her reservations. She had loved rehearsing, especially enjoying the lively company of the other amateur actors. The evening had been full of laughter and a growing sense of shared purpose.

"Way to go, Mom," Zoe said, giving her a high five as she ran out the door to catch her ride.

"Break a leg," Sara muttered, offering the traditional advice as she poured herself a cup of coffee and carried it back up to her room where she was working on a paper.

"I guess I won't be seeing much of you," Bill said, poking his egg with a fork and making the yolk run out. "What with rehearsals and all."

"I've put the schedule on the fridge," Lucy said, spreading some marmalade on an English muffin. "Rehearsals are seven to nine most evenings." She took a bite and chewed. "It's not like we even talk to each other much after dinner, anyway. You usually do fantasy football on the computer and I watch TV. It will be good to shake things up a bit."

"I suppose," he said mournfully.

Lucy chuckled. "I think you're the actor in the family."

Bill had the good grace to blush. "I will miss you," he said.

"Come to the rehearsals, then. You could help backstage."

He was quick to come up with a reason to stay home.

"Someone should keep an eye on the girls," he said, wiping his plate with his toast.

As Lucy tidied the kitchen she set her mind to considering who might be willing to buy an ad. Most of her friends were watching their pennies with Christmas taking up any spare change. Her old friend Miss Tilley was a possibility, until Lucy remembered that Rachel had probably already asked her. Who, she wondered, as she wiped the counters, was likely to support local theater?

She was rinsing out the sponge when she remembered a series of articles she wrote in September profiling local people with surprising hobbies. The fire chief, Buzz Bresnahan, was a theater buff who traveled to New York City a couple of times a year to see Broadway shows. And his daughter, Alison, was studying theater at Ohio University. Deciding he would be her first target, she dried her hands and reached for her jacket, intending to make her first stop of the day at the fire station.

But when she arrived at the station the ambulance was pulling out of its bay, lights flashing and siren wailing.

She ran inside and caught the dispatcher's eye. "What's up?"

"Medical assistance at Downeast Mortgage," Krissy Kirwan replied, one of Dot's numerous offspring who worked in public safety. "Sounds like a heart attack."

Maybe it was news, maybe it wasn't, Lucy mused. There was only one way to find out, so she got in her car and followed the ambulance down Main Street to the Downeast Mortgage office. The office was in a neat little brick building that had once housed a bank. Stone steps with black wrought iron railings led to a plate glass door, with a window on either side. The ambulance took up most of the small parking lot, so Lucy parked on the street. She hurried to the door, hoping she could slip inside without being noticed, because she knew from previous experience that the rescue team didn't appreciate an audience.

She was just reaching the stone steps when the door flew open and Ben Scribner flew out. From his wailing you would have thought the hounds of hell were pursuing him instead of his faithful secretary Elsie Morehouse.

"You'll freeze out here, Mr. Scribner," she begged him. "Come back inside."

Scribner was standing in the inch or so of snow that was on the ground, shivering in the light sweater he wore over his oxford cloth shirt and khaki pants. His thinning white hair was standing straight up on his head, his eyes were wide with fear, and a line of saliva was dribbling down his chin. "No! No! Get away!"

A couple of EMTs had appeared in the doorway behind Elsie, and a police cruiser was just arriving. "It's just me, Mr. Scribner. Elsie."

Scribner shook his head; he was trembling violently. "Jake Marlowe was here," he said. "I saw him. In the flesh."

Barney Culpepper was getting out of his cruiser and assessing the situation, unobserved by Scribner.

"Now, now." Elsie's voice was soothing. "You know perfectly well that Mr. Marlowe is dead. He died in the fire."

"He did!" Scribner's head was jerking up and down like a bobble-head doll's.

"I know he did. He's dead as a doornail. But he was here! He's come back from the dead."

"That's impossible, Mr. Scribner. You must have imagined it."

"He told me . . ."

"What did he tell you?" Elsie asked, keeping eye contact with Scribner and ignoring Barney's approach, even though she was aware of it.

"He was w-w-warning me."

A female EMT unfolded a red blanket, which she offered to Scribner. "Let me put this around you, warm you up," she said.

"Fire! Fire!" Scribner pointed to the blanket and stepped backward, shivering violently.

The EMT advanced with the blanket and Scribner scuttled backward, right into the officer's waiting arms. Barney had him cuffed and confined to the back of his cruiser in a smooth, practiced sequence of moves. Then they were off, headed to the emergency room. The other rescuers began leaving and Lucy approached Elsie Morehouse.

"Are you all right?" she asked. "That was pretty intense."

"Mr. Scribner's very upset about losing his partner." Elsie had a sweater over her shoulders and her arms were folded defensively across her chest.

"Let's go inside and get you warm," Lucy urged. She fully expected Elsie to tell her to scram, and was surprised when the secretary allowed herself to be led inside. A full coffeepot was sitting on a credenza and Lucy poured a cup, adding a couple of sugars and some milk.

"Drink this," she said, and Elsie sat right down like a good little girl and took the mug.

"Did anything in particular set him off?" Lucy asked.

"Mr. Scribner thought he saw Mr. Marlowe's ghost. At first he wasn't afraid, but it seems he didn't like what Mr. Marlowe told him. That's when he got so upset."

"Did he say what Mr. Marlowe told him?" Lucy asked.

Elsie was holding the mug with both hands, and though she was obviously distressed, her makeup and pixie cut hair were perfect. "He was babbling, but I think the gist of it was that if he didn't change his ways the same thing would happen to him. I guess he meant the explosion." She gulped some coffee. "It was all in Mr. Scribner's head, of course. He had some sort of fantasy or hallucination. That's it." She narrowed her eyes. "You're from the paper, aren't you?"

"Uh, yes," Lucy admitted.

"Well, thank you very much for fixing the coffee, but I think you better leave now. And anything you saw here is off the record." She glared at Lucy. "Understood?"

"What you told me is off the record," Lucy said. "But everything that happened outside took place in public and involved town employees. I can and will report it."

"Well, I never," Elsie sniffed, her lips pursed in disapproval. "That's a disgusting way to behave."

"Oh," Lucy responded, her ire rising. "I suppose you think it's perfectly fine to foreclose and make families homeless. That's a nice thing to do?"

Elsie was holding the door for her, indicating she should leave, now. But first she wanted to get in the last word. "You can't let people walk away from their obligations," she said, bristling with righteous indignation. "Think of the moral hazard."

"Moral hazard," Lucy repeated, stepping outside into the frosty morning air. "That's a new one on me."

Chapter Four

"Moral hazard," Lucy repeated, muttering to herself. She'd been hearing that term a lot lately. What on earth did it mean? Could it possibly mean that, if for some reason a borrower couldn't meet his obligations, he would somehow be morally at risk if the creditor adjusted the terms of the loan? That a borrower's morality would be preserved if his family became homeless, rather than if he received a month or two of forbearance?

She thought of Lexie and Zach Cunningham, who were struggling to keep their home and provide medical care for their daughter, and wondered how the theory of moral hazard could possibly apply to them. Their debt would be satisfied if Downeast repossessed their home, but what about their parental obligation to provide shelter for their children? It wasn't Lexie's fault that her hours were cut because of the recession—that was completely out of her control. What were they to do? They had increased expenses because she'd lost her employer-subsidized health care at the same time their income was reduced. That was a simple enough equation to

Lucy, but apparently the Ben Scribners and Elsie More-houses of this world saw it differently. To them the inability to pay all one's bills, a situation commonly known as poverty, was not simply an economic crisis but was a moral one, too.

But what about the lessons she'd learned in Sunday School? She remembered contributing a quarter each week to "help the poor" and had never forgotten that most important Golden Rule: "Do unto others as you would have others do unto you." She was in her car now, driving down the street past several Downeast FOR SALE signs, trying to understand how all these foreclosures could possibly benefit anyone. Families were dislocated, forced to leave their homes and find shelter where they could. The town was losing citizens, sometimes people whose families had made their homes in Tinker's Cove for centuries. And even Ben Scribner must have realized that accumulating a number of properties that nobody could afford to buy was hardly a good business policy.

She found herself wondering about Scribner and Marlowe, and their relationship. It seemed it might have been somewhat strained, considering Scribner's reaction to his dead partner's reappearance. According to Elsie, Marlowe had warned Scribner that he was going to meet a fiery end, just as he did. But from what she'd seen, it seemed that Scribner was actually terrified of his deceased partner. Why should that be? she wondered, turning into the parking area behind the *Pennysaver* office. They'd been partners for decades, the company was a fixture in town, and the two men had always seemed to be of similar minds. Why should Scribner suddenly be afraid of his longtime partner? Lucy could think of only one reason: guilt. If Scribner had a guilty conscience he might well fear the return of a revenge-seeking Jake Marlowe.

Ted and Phyllis were already at work when Lucy arrived. "You're late," Ted said, glancing at the clock. It wasn't a criticism, merely an observation.

"There was an emergency at Downeast Mortgage and I went to see what it was all about," she explained, hanging up her coat.

"Another explosion?" Phyllis asked.

"No, nothing like that. Ben Scribner had a panic attack, that's all."

"Understandable, I guess," Ted said. "He must be feeling kind of paranoid. After all, the fire that killed Marlowe was started by a bomb, disguised as a Christmas package."

Lucy sat down with a thud in her desk chair. "I think that is so mean," she said.

"Yeah," Phyllis agreed, with a nod that shook her double chin. "Sending a bomb is bad enough, but wrapping it up in Christmas paper is . . . Well, I don't know exactly what it is, but it's not nice."

"Really not nice," Lucy said. "It kind of makes you feel bad for poor old Marlowe. He was such a miser, he was probably really excited about getting a present."

"For a minute or two he must have thought somebody actually liked him," Phyllis said.

"Which really wasn't the case," Lucy mused. "He wasn't very popular."

"Truth is, he worked pretty hard to make himself unpopular," Phyllis added.

"Ahem." Ted cleared his throat. "If you ladies don't mind, we have work to do."

They both fell silent and folded their hands in their laps, waiting for instructions.

"Phyllis, this is a list of advertisers who haven't renewed their contracts. I want you to call them, offer them these new reduced rates for our holiday issues." He handed her a couple of sheets of paper, then turned to Lucy. "As for you, Lucy, I want you to check the legal ads for the last year or so and find out how many people have actually lost their homes to Downeast Mortgage. Once you get the properties you'll have to follow up at the Registry of Deeds."

"Sounds like you're planning a big story," Lucy said.

"We'll see," Ted said. "Let's find out the facts first."

This was the sort of assignment Lucy loved. There was nothing better than digging through old papers for nuggets of truth. She loved the big, oversized volumes of bound papers that went back over a hundred years to the days of the old *Courier and Advertiser*. It was unfortunate, in her opinion, that Ted had switched to digitized versions of the more recent papers. She loved leafing through the brown and brittle pages that revealed past times: ads for corsets and transistor radios and cans of Campbell's tomato soup for ten cents. Not that the computer versions didn't have advantages. The computer wasn't dusty, for one thing, and it was a lot easier and faster to find what you were looking for.

By lunchtime, Lucy had made an interesting discovery. Not only had Downeast Mortgage foreclosed on dozens of homes in the county, at least one of those properties was owned by a town employee.

Harbormaster Harry Crawford stood to lose the remaining hundred and twenty acres of his family's waterfront farm, a property that the Crawfords had held for at least two hundred years. Lucy was willing to bet the amount owed on the mortgage was a mere fraction of what that property was worth. It was prime waterfront, perfect for a resort.

As the afternoon wore on Lucy discovered Crawford wasn't the only town employee to lose a unique piece of property. It seemed that Downeast Mortgage stood to profit handsomely from Marlowe's FinCom vote to reduce town employees' hours. Assistant building inspector Phil Watkins had lost his LEED-certified green home. Lucy remembered writing a story about the house, which had special shingles equipped with solar cells that provided electricity. Watkins had boasted that the house produced so much electricity, in fact, that his meter ran backward and the electric company was paying him. He'd been terribly proud of that fact and Lucy knew he must be heartbroken about losing his energy-efficient home.

Health department secretary Annie Kraus's loss wasn't so remarkable; her home was a simple two-bedroom ranch. Nothing fancy or special about it, except that it was her home. Natural resources officer Nelson Macmillan also lost his property, but it was only a building lot, probably bought as an investment. Or maybe he'd dreamed of building himself the perfect house there one day.

Lucy stared at the list she'd made and sighed. It seemed a sad record of shattered hopes and diminished dreams. She remembered when she and Bill had first moved to Tinker's Cove and settled into the ramshackle handyman's special they'd bought on Red Top Road. The place had a failing furnace, cracked walls and ceilings, peeling wallpaper, and no insulation in the walls except for seaweed and newspaper. She remembered going into baby Toby's nursery one morning and finding him cozy and warm in his footed sleeper, sound asleep in his crib, the covers dusted with snow that had blown through a gap in the wall. They'd worked hard, scraping and painting and repairing, and turned the old house into a cozy, attractive, comfortable home that was now worth many times what they originally paid for it. But it wasn't the thought of profit that had motivated them, it was the desire to make a home for their growing family.

When Lucy finally emerged from the morgue the office was empty and it was dark outside; as often happened when she did research, she'd lost track of the time. It was nearly five according to the regulator clock that hung on the wall above Ted's desk. She had to get a move on if she wasn't going to be late for rehearsal. When she got home she discovered Bill had dinner well in hand and was frying up hamburgers. Even so, the rehearsal was in full swing when she arrived at the Community Church, where some twenty or so cast members were sitting around a table.

" 'Are there no workhouses?' " Bob was reading from the script. " 'Has the treadmill stopped its useful work?' "

"Ah, Lucy, you're here," Rachel interjected. "Before I forget, I need to measure you for your costume. . . . What did I do with that tape measure? Let's take ten."

While Rachel searched for the tape measure, Lucy got settled, removing her coat and taking the seat at the table indicated by a copy of the script with her name in big block letters. There was also a bottle of water so she took a few sips while she flipped through the pages, looking for the scene they were reading. When she found the line Bob had been reading, she smiled. "Bob, I had no idea you'd be such a terrific Scrooge," she said.

"Isn't he wonderful?" Florence asked, leaning forward in such a way that her blouse fell open, revealing a good bit of lacy black bra. "I had no idea he could be so downright mean!"

There was something in the way she was batting her eyelashes, something in the almost Southern accent that had crept into her voice, that made Lucy wonder if this was *Gone with the Wind* rather than *A Christmas Carol*.

"Bob has hidden talents," Rachel said in a rather snappish voice. "Stand up, Lucy," she ordered, leading her away from the group for a modicum of privacy and slipping the tape around her bust. "I'm beginning to have second thoughts about Florence," she whispered, making a notation of the measurement.

Florence and Bob had their heads together on the opposite side of the table and were chuckling about something; Florence had her hand on Bob's arm.

"She's just friendly," Lucy replied. "Very friendly."

"I'm keeping an eye on her," Rachel whispered, turning to welcome another late comer. "Hi, Al," she said, waving at a middle-aged man who was wearing overalls under a plaid shirt-jacket and was carrying a toolbox. "Everybody, this is Al Roberts. He's going to be building our set."

Al set down his toolbox and gave everyone a wave. "I've got some drawings," he said, pulling some folded papers out of his pocket.

"Great," Rachel enthused. "Let's take a look at 'em."

Al took off his watch cap, revealing a very bald head, and came over to the table, where he spread out the drawings, then pushed his black-framed glasses back up his nose. "The way I see it," he began, "is three flats with different motifs. One is kind of domestic, suggesting paneling and a fireplace, for the interior scenes. Another flat will suggest Scrooge's office, and the third will be a sort of street scene, with a window that opens, for the scene when Scrooge discovers it's Christmas morning. The idea is that we leave them all in place for the entire show but highlight the appropriate backdrop with lighting."

"This is brilliant," Rachel said. "I love that it's so economical."

"You can add props as needed...." Al suggested. "You know, a high desk and a stool for Bob Cratchit, a street lamp for the exterior scenes, a kitchen table for the Cratchit household, a four-poster for Scrooge..." He paused. "The only problem is, I'm not much of an artist. I can build the flats but somebody else has got to do the painting."

"Oh, I can do that," Florence volunteered.

"Florence is an artist, you know," Bob said, beaming at her. "She illustrates children's books."

"Great," Rachel said with a curt nod.

"Well, that's fine then." Al rose and gathered up his papers. "I'll get started tomorrow." He turned to Rachel. "Is there any problem getting in here? Do I need a key or anything?"

"It's usually open," she said. "If you're getting the lumber delivered, I think you better set that up with the church office. There are other activities here. The Ladies Aid probably wouldn't want their meeting interrupted."

"They might have tightened things up," Bob suggested. "After the fire, I mean."

The group of actors seated around the table all nodded gravely, and there were murmurs of "terrible" and "shocking."

"People are far too casual about safety," Marge offered. "My Barney's always telling me that folks don't lock their doors—they even leave the keys in the car and then they wonder how it got stolen."

"Locking the door wouldn't have helped Jake Marlowe," Lucy said.

"If you ask me, he got no more than what he deserved," Al said.

"What do you mean?" Florence demanded in a confrontational tone.

"Just that what goes around comes around," Al said. "He treated a lot of people badly, plus he didn't even take care of his own place, that's all. It's not exactly a secret."

Florence nodded. "I know, you're right. I told my uncle, that house was a fire waiting to happen."

"Your uncle?" Lucy asked.

"Ben Scribner. He's my uncle." There was a sort of embarrassed silence and Florence hurried to fill it. "He's scared witless, you know. He won't touch the mail. He's terrified he'll be next."

"I wouldn't be surprised if he was," Al said under his breath, as he put his hat on and pulled his gloves out of his pocket. "Like I said, I'll start on the scenery tomorrow—that's if everything works out with the delivery." He raised his gloves in a salute and turned to go.

"Okay, everyone," Rachel said, clapping her hands. "Back to work. Act one, scene three. Your line, Bob."

Chapter Five

"So how was the rehearsal?" Bill asked on Saturday morning.

Lucy was sitting at the round golden oak table in her kitchen, a steaming mug of coffee in front of her, looking out the window. It wasn't an inspiring view on this cloudy morning. The trees were bare and the ground muddy from melting snow. A bright red male cardinal and a couple of chickadees were pecking hopefully at the empty bird feeder, and she made a mental note to fill it.

"It was just a read-through but it went really well. Bob is really talented; he's going to be a great Scrooge. And the guy who's playing Marley's ghost is a real hoot. He moans and wails: 'Mankind was my business. The common welfare was my business.' When he gets those chains rattling he's going to be really terrifying."

"So this is going to be a PG performance, too scary for Patrick," Bill said, filling his mug.

"What's too scary for Patrick?" Sara asked, shuffling across the kitchen floor in her fuzzy slippers and opening the fridge.

"I was just saying that the actor playing Marley's

ghost is awfully good," Lucy explained. "And believe me, nothing has changed in the fridge since yesterday, so grab a yogurt and shut the door."

"Why don't you get the good yogurt?" Sara complained, reaching for the orange juice. "The stuff you buy is full of chemicals."

"It's light—it's only got ninety calories," Lucy said.

"You should buy the Greek kind. It's natural."

"It costs twice as much," Lucy said.

Sara slumped down in the chair opposite Lucy's and stared at her glass of juice. Bill pulled the frying pan out of the cupboard, making a clatter, and she covered her ears with her hands. "Do you have to make such a racket?"

Just then Zoe came thumping down the stairs in her boots. "Where's my French book?" she demanded in a loud voice. "Who took my French book?"

"It's where you left it, stupid," Sara growled. "And what do you need it for, anyway? It's Saturday, moron. There's no school, and why are you yelling?"

"Don't call me stupid," Zoe snarled. "I've got a study group meeting to work on a project for French class— Christmas in France—and I wasn't yelling."

"I think it's in the family room, on the coffee table. And, yes, Zoe, you were yelling. And, Sara, there's no need to be insulting." Lucy narrowed her eyes, remembering that when she went to bed last night Sara was still out. "Do you have a hangover?" she asked suspiciously.

"No!" Sara was outraged. "Why do you think that?"

"Just because you're awfully sensitive this morning." Lucy paused, watching as Bill started frying himself a couple of eggs. "You're under age—you shouldn't be drinking."

"I wasn't." Sara wrinkled her nose and stuck out her tongue at Zoe, who was stuffing her French book into her book bag.

Lucy turned her attention to her youngest. "Do you want some breakfast?"

"No. We're meeting at the doughnut shop," she replied, hearing a beep from outside and grabbing her parka. "Gotta go. See you later."

"I wish she'd eat breakfast," Lucy sighed, making sure the door was shut.

"I wish she'd go away," Sara muttered.

"What do you mean by that?" Bill demanded, sitting down at the table and glaring at Sara.

"Oh, nothing. She's just so annoying. So juvenile."

Lucy's and Bill's eyes met for a moment, then Bill dug into his breakfast, poking an egg with his fork and making the bright yellow yolk run out onto his toast. He popped a big piece into his mouth.

"Are you buying free range eggs, Mom?" Sara asked. "You should, you know. Those chicken farms are cruel. The hens are kept cooped up in cages, and they never get outside to act like chickens."

"I buy what's on sale," Lucy said. "Which reminds me, Bill. There's an opening on the FinCom now that Marlowe's no longer with us, and Pam was saying she thinks you would be the right person to fill it."

Bill swallowed. "How exactly did a discussion about eggs lead you to the FinCom vacancy?"

"It's obvious," Lucy said, shrugging. "I was thinking about the price of eggs and how expensive things are these days, and I was doing some research yesterday about town employees losing their homes because their hours have been cut by the FinCom. . . ."

"Yeah, rents are really crazy," Sara volunteered. "They've gone sky high."

Lucy and Bill both stared at her. "Rents?" they asked in chorus.

"What do you know about rents?" Bill demanded.

"Are you planning to move out?" Lucy asked.

"Well, sure," Sara admitted. "Of course I want to move out."

"You do?" Lucy asked.

"Why?" asked Bill.

"Because . . . I'm in college. I don't want to be living with my parents. I want to be independent."

"I know, it's tough," Lucy agreed. "But tuition is so high, we can't afford room and board, too. That's why Winchester is perfect. It's right here in town. And they gave you a good deal with that local student scholarship."

"Being a townie is like being in high school," Sara complained. "If I went in with some friends and got a job, a part-time job, I could afford an apartment. At least I thought I could. But the rents have really gone up. Amy and I looked at a place yesterday but it was over seven hundred dollars a month. And it was a dump! The bathroom was all moldy and the kitchen was really icky."

"I don't want you getting a job," Bill said. "Your grades will suffer."

"Most of the businesses around here are laying people off," Lucy added.

"I know," Sara admitted. "I stopped in at Fern's Famous Fudge the other day to see if I could get my old job back, but Dora said she was sorry but she doesn't need any help."

"Jobs are getting scarcer than hen's teeth," Lucy said.

"Now you're back to chickens," Bill said, wiping his plate with his last bit of toast.

"So what about the FinCom?" Lucy asked, pressing the issue.

"I'll think about it," Bill conceded.

"I think they need somebody like you. Right now they're tied. Pam and Frankie think town services are important, but the other two, the men, are budget cutters."

"What do you mean, *somebody like me*? Do you think I'll automatically join the tax-and-spend faction that wants to run the town into bankruptcy?"

"Well, you wouldn't vote to cut things, would you?" Sara demanded. "Not when so many people are suffering."

"Those needy people have to pay taxes, too," Bill replied. "What's the good of, say, keeping town hall open forty hours a week if it means people can't afford to pay their taxes?"

"But those cuts mean a lot of town employees can't keep their homes," Lucy said. "That's not good for the town's economy, either."

"Yeah!" Sara chimed in, glaring at her father. "The one percent is getting rich and the ninety-nine percent are fighting over the scraps, trying to survive."

Bill raised his hands in a sign of surrender. "I'm just saying being on the FinCom is a big responsibility, and if I do it I'm going to make up my own mind. It's a balancing act—I'm very aware of that—and I won't go in with a preconceived agenda."

Lucy was stuffing plates in the dishwasher. "Well, what's the point of doing it if you're not going to change things?"

"Yeah, Dad. Mom's right."

Bill grabbed his jacket off the hook and stared at them, as if he was about to say something. Apparently thinking better of it, he jammed his hat on his head and went out the door, letting it slam behind him.

"I wish you wouldn't upset your father like that," Lucy said, shutting the dishwasher.

"Me?" Sara's voice rose in pitch. "He's not mad at me. He's mad at you." She got up, leaving her empty juice glass on the table. "But don't give up, Mom. Seth says we've got to fight for our rights."

Then she was climbing the stairs to her room and Lucy picked up the glass and put it in the dishwasher. "I'm not your maid," she muttered, thinking, and not for the first time, that there ought to be a labor union for mothers.

In fact, that's what she said to Pam, when she met her later that morning. The two had agreed to spend the day selling ads in the show program to local businesses. Lucy hadn't sold her quota yet and was eager to get it done.

"A labor union for mothers, that's a really good idea," Pam said.

"We'd work to code. We'd have defined duties. No picking up after husbands and children. We'd demand they empty their pockets before putting clothes in the wash. . . ."

"And unroll their socks," Pam added.

"And if they didn't, we'd fine them," Lucy suggested.

"I like that idea," Pam said, smiling.

"You don't think I'm serious," Lucy said.

"Oh, I think you're serious, all right. But I don't think this idea will fly."

"It's a good idea, though," Lucy said, as they went into the liquor store where the clerk, Cliff Sandstrom, greeted them with a smile.

After asking about his family, Pam produced the program for last year's show, open to the full page ad Wine and Dine had taken out then. "The rates are the same—fifty dollars for a full page—and if you throw in another ten, which will go to the Angel Fund, you'll get a little angel printed in the corner."

Cliff seemed doubtful. "Angel Fund?"

"That's for Angie Cunningham. She lives here in town. She's got juvenile polycystic kidney disease and her family's having a rough time coping with medical expenses."

"Oh, right. I know Lexie. She said her hours have been cut."

"She doesn't work enough hours to get health insurance now."

"Doesn't she get COBRA?" he asked.

"Yeah, but she has to pay double what she's used to."

Cliff looked thoughtful. "That's tough," he said. "Look, I'll have to cut down the ad. I can only afford a quarter page this year." He opened the cash drawer and pulled out a couple of bills. "And here's five for the little girl. I wish I could do more."

"Every little bit helps," Lucy said. "Thank you."

"I've got a little girl Angie's age," Cliff said. "I'd go crazy if anything happened to her."

"I know how you feel," Pam said, writing out a receipt. "Thanks again."

The two friends worked their way along the street, but the story was the same everywhere. People wished they could do more, but this year they had to cut back. When Pam and Lucy reached the end of the street Lucy had satisfied her hundred dollar ad quota but had only raised twenty dollars for the Angel Fund. Next up, on the other side, was Downeast Mortgage.

"I don't know if Elsie will even let us talk to Scribner," Lucy said, as they crossed the street. "She's a bit of a pit bull."

"With lipstick?" Pam asked mischievously.

"And eye shadow, too."

But when they stepped inside the mortgage company's office, they found Elsie's desk empty. Apparently even Scribner didn't expect her to work on Saturday—or he was too cheap to pay overtime. He was there, however, working at his desk and keeping an eye on the reception area through the open door.

"What do you want?" he asked in a brusque tone, without looking up.

"Good morning," Lucy said in a cheery voice.

"Season's greetings," Pam added.

"It's not a good morning and I don't observe the season," Scribner said, making a note on the sheaf of papers he was studying. "And I don't have time to waste."

"We won't take much of your time," Lucy said, stepping into the doorway, but not daring to go further without an invitation to enter his office.

"And we're very sorry about your loss," Pam added, joining her.

"Me, too, and now I've got twice as much work to do." He furrowed his bristly, untamed brows and glared at them through his wire-rimmed glasses. "Now, for the second time, what brings you here?"

"We're from the Community Players," Lucy began. "They're putting on *A Christmas Carol* this year—I'm actually playing Mrs. Cratchit—and we're selling ads in the show program. For fifty dollars . . ."

Scribner turned a page. "Not interested," he said, with a dismissive wave of his hand.

"This year is a little different," Pam said, taking a step forward. "The show is a fund-raiser for Angie Cunningham. She's a little girl who lives here in town and has polycystic kidney disease. Her family is struggling with high medical expenses. It's very difficult in this economy—"

"What business is that of mine?" Scribner demanded.

"Well, they're your neighbors," Lucy said, also taking a baby step forward and standing next to Pam. "They live here in town. And they're customers of yours. Surely it's in your interest to help them."

Scribner folded his hands on his desk and leaned forward. "My interest is charging interest—that's what I do." He laughed. "And I pay plenty in taxes, most of which goes to so-called *entitlements*." He spit out the last word, as if it left a bad taste in his mouth. "What about Medicaid? And there's that children's health program, CHIP or SHIP or something. They should apply for that."

"I don't know the details," Lucy confessed.

"Those programs are worthy efforts, but they don't cover everything," Pam said. "And there are strict eligibility requirements."

"And so there should be!" Scribner exclaimed, smacking his fist down hard on his desk. "People have to take some responsibility for themselves, don't they? There are far too many freeloaders! Do you know half of the population doesn't even pay income tax? The government actually pays them! Earned Income Credit! How is that right?"

"There's a certain minimum people need to survive," Lucy said. "People who qualify for the Earned Income Credit make very little money indeed."

"Well, they should work harder then!" Scribner thundered. "Make 'em work for their benefits. Put 'em on the roads, picking up trash."

"I take it you're not interested in buying an ad," Pam said.

"You'd be right." Scribner revealed his teeth in something that was more like a grimace than a smile.

"And I presume you don't want to donate to the Angel Fund," Lucy said.

"Exactly right."

"We won't bother you further," Pam said.

"Good." Scribner dismissed them with a curt nod and they left, practically on tiptoes, closing the door quietly behind them.

Back outside, they shivered and pulled on their gloves.

"Wow, what a cheapskate," Lucy said.

"We shouldn't be judgmental," Pam said. She taught yoga and had studied Eastern religions. "He's having a difficult time coping with his loss."

"You'd think that would make him more understanding of others' problems, more compassionate."

"Grief takes everyone differently," Pam said.

"He didn't seem grief stricken to me," Lucy said. "He

seemed put out that his partner died and left him with a lot of extra work to do."

"You could be right," Pam admitted, pausing in front of Fern's Famous Fudge. "I hear that all the time, you know. If people are poor it's their own fault—they should just work harder. But there's only so many hours in the day and wages have gone down, not up, in the past few years, and that's if you can even get a job."

"I blame those big box stores," Lucy said.

"You've got a point. They pay minimum wage and they don't give any benefits, and worst of all, they don't give people a full week's worth of hours. They keep them on call, have them come in when they need them, which means they can't get a second job because they don't know when they'll be called to work."

Lucy bit her lip, thinking this sounded a lot like her working conditions at the *Pennysaver*. Pam's husband, Ted, didn't offer health insurance, and she and Phyllis often joked that their wages made them more like volunteers than employees.

"I know," Lucy said. "People used to make a living working in the local stores, but those little businesses can't compete with the national chains."

"Look at the empty storefronts," Pam said, with a wave of her hand. "The Mad Hatter, Chanticleer Chocolates, Mainely Books—they're all gone."

Lucy lowered her voice and nodded toward the pink and white striped curtains that hung in the windows at Fern's Famous. "Sara told me this morning she went in to see if they needed help for the holidays and Dora told her business is so bad she can't use her."

"Tell me about it," Pam moaned. "Ads are down at the *Pennysaver*. Fern's Famous cut their budget, and a lot of businesses aren't advertising at all. Ted's really worried. He doesn't know how much longer he can keep going."

Lucy's heart skipped a beat and her tummy tightened. As much as she complained about her working conditions, she loved her job. She couldn't imagine her life without it. "That's awful," was all she could say.

"Oh, don't worry. He's been drawing on the home equity line to make up the difference." Pam laughed. "We'll be fine as long as this recession doesn't go on too long." She paused, pulling the door open and holding it for Lucy. "And if real estate values recover."

"Hi, ladies," Dora said, greeting them from her spot behind the counter. "What can I do for you?"

Lucy inhaled the warm, seductive scent of chocolate and gazed at the vintage picture that hung on the wall as Pam launched into her spiel. If only life was like that picture, full of sunshine and chocolate and smiling cows and apple-cheeked children. But it looked as if it was going to be a long, hard winter in Tinker's Cove this year.

Chapter Six

When Lucy got to the office on Monday, Phyllis was at her desk but Ted hadn't come in yet. She didn't hesitate to unburden herself of the disturbing knowledge that had bothered her all weekend, following Pam's admission of financial trouble.

"I was out selling ads for the Community Players' program with Pam on Saturday," she began, unwinding her scarf and removing her jacket. "She told me some pretty scary stuff about our jobs."

Phyllis smoothed her sparkly, beaded cardigan over her significant bust and leaned forward, propping her elbows on her desk. "Really? What did she say?"

Lucy went over to the chest-high reception counter that separated Phyllis's work space from the rest of the office. "She said Ted is borrowing against their home equity line to keep the *Pennysaver* going—and she doesn't know how long they can keep doing it."

The thin lines that were all that remained of Phyllis's eyebrows rose above her reading glasses and she nodded, causing her double chins to quiver. "Now that you mention it, I'm not surprised. Ads have been way down."

She plucked a copy of the *Pennysaver* from the pile on the counter. "See how thin it is? That's because there's hardly any ads. He's even got a full page house ad touting lower ad rates."

"I feel really stupid," Lucy admitted. "Here I'm supposed to be a reporter and I never noticed. I've been so wrapped up in Christmas and the show and the kids I didn't notice what was going on right under my nose. Now it turns out I might not have a job—and at Christmas, too."

"That's when the pink slips always come out, which is pretty ironic if you ask me," Phyllis said.

"Right. Just when people's budgets are stretched to the max buying presents and fancy food and all the Christmas stuff. Even the electric bill goes sky high, what with all the lights."

Phyllis's expression was thoughtful as she examined her freshly manicured nails, done in Christmasy red and green stripes. "But if you're realistic, it's not much of a job," she said in a consoling tone. "My pay barely covers my manis and hair appointments."

Lucy scowled, acknowledging that she had a valid point. "If I get some overtime my check might cover the week's groceries and a tank of gas—but it's my job and I like it."

"I know. It's kind of fun. . . ." Phyllis paused, then added, "Some of the time. But face it, I can't remember the last time we got raises. And there's no benefits, none. It's not a real job like Wilf has with health insurance and a pension plan."

"I hate to rain on your parade," Lucy said, "but the postal service is in trouble, too. They're talking about huge layoffs."

"They'll work it out, they always do," Phyllis said, adding a long sigh. "Frankly, I'd be more than happy if he would take early retirement. I've been sick with worry ever since that bomb. He must've delivered it, you know. He handled it. What if it went off? It could've been him who got killed and not mean old Jake Marlowe."

Just then the little bell on the door jangled and Ted marched in, apparently full of vim and vigor. "What's up? How come you're gossiping? Don't you have any work to do?"

"Just keeping our fingers on the pulse of news in Tinker's Cove," Lucy said, hurrying over to her desk.

"And what exactly is so interesting this morning?" Ted asked, stuffing his gloves in the pocket of his parka.

"Cuts in postal service," Lucy said. "I think we ought to interview the postmaster, see what the effect would be. Talk to Country Cousins—they send out all those catalogs."

Ted hung up his coat on the old-fashioned stand that tipped this way and that with each new addition. "Actually, that's a good idea, Lucy. Why don't you get on it?"

"Righto," Lucy said, booting up her computer. While it clicked and groaned with the effort of turning itself on, she wished she'd kept her mouth shut. Now, in addition to the town committee meetings that she routinely covered, she also had two stories that required a lot of research: foreclosures and postal cuts. Sighing, she reached for the phone, dialing the post office. She was listening to it ring, unanswered, when Wilf Lundgren arrived with the morning mail.

"Hi, sweetie," he greeted his wife, setting the bundle, neatly fastened with a big rubber band, on the counter.

"Hi, yourself," she said, slipping the band off and giving it back to him. "You can use this again."

"Sure will," he said, beaming at her. Wilf had a round face and his cheeks were red from the cold; he was wearing the regulation blue gray postal uniform. "How's your day been so far?"

"Looking better now that you're here," she replied, with a wink.

"Cut it out, you two," Ted groaned. "You're making me sick."

"Party pooper," Phyllis snapped. She turned to Wilf. "Have you got a date for lunch?"

"Do now," Wilf said, turning to go.

"Hold on," Lucy cried. "Don't go. I need to talk to the postmaster, but nobody's answering the phone."

Wilf adopted a concerned expression. "What for? Do you have a complaint?"

"No, no. I'm just doing a story about these proposed service cuts, that's all."

"I can give you the postmaster's private line, but you've got to promise not to say I gave it to you," he said.

Lucy jotted it down. "Thanks."

Ted was pouring himself a cup of coffee. "How's everybody holding up over there?" he asked, taking a long drink. "Are they worried?"

Wilf shrugged and shifted his heavy bag from one shoulder to the other. "Trying not to," he said. "It's out of our control. There's nothing we can do about it. It's like that bomb that I delivered to Marlowe. It coulda gone off in my bag—lucky for me it didn't. Maybe we'll get lucky and keep our jobs. Maybe we won't."

"Oh, don't talk about it!" Phyllis exclaimed, with a

shudder. "It makes me crazy just to think about that thing going off."

"Yeah," Lucy agreed. "It's scary to think anybody could wrap up an explosive and mail it."

"You said it. It looked like a Christmas present. Even had a *Do Not Open Till Christmas* label." Wilf shoved out his lower lip. "He should've waited; he'd still be alive if he hadn't been such a greedy bastard."

"This isn't the first time there have been mail bombs," Lucy said. "And there was that anthrax scare. People don't realize that being a postal worker is so risky."

"It's the first time we ever had a package bomb here in Tinker's Cove and I sure hope it's the last," Wilf said, glancing at the regulator clock on the wall and heading for the door. "I gotta get going. I'm behind my schedule." He tipped his hat to Phyllis and added a wink. "See you later, babe."

Lucy was laughing; she'd thrown her head back and sent her wheeled desk chair scooting backward. "He's wild about you, Phyllis!" she hooted.

Phyllis pursed her lips primly, but her cheeks had gone quite pink. "Our anniversary's coming up."

"How long is it now?" Ted asked.

"Four years."

"And you're still like newlyweds," Lucy said.

"It's true," Phyllis said, as the fax machine went into action with a whirring sound. "I think it's because we married late. I don't think either one of us ever thought we'd find the right one."

"I guess you were smart to wait," Lucy said, as Phyllis handed her the fax.

"It's from the funeral home. Marlowe's memorial service is Friday afternoon."

"I don't imagine there's much of a body since he was already cremated in the fire," Ted said, causing the two women to groan.

"Who's paying for it?" Lucy wondered. "I don't think Marlowe had any family and I can't imagine Scribner would spend a penny he didn't absolutely have to."

"Unlikely," Ted agreed.

"There won't be much of a spread," Phyllis predicted. "Probably nothing but tea punch and lemon cookies. I don't know if it's worth going. There probably won't be much of a turnout. Marlowe wasn't very popular."

"Maybe not," Lucy said, "but chances are whoever sent that bomb will be there, and I'm going to be there, too."

"I don't think the bomber will be wearing a sign, Lucy, and your week is filling up," Ted said, going through his e-mails. "The state fire marshal's holding a press conference tomorrow morning, in Augusta. I've got that publishers' conference, so you'll have to cover it."

"What time?" Lucy asked, thinking she would need at least an hour to drive to the state's capitol.

"Ten."

"That's not too bad, but it will take most of the morning. I don't think I'll have time for those feature stories."

"Next week, then," Ted said, uncharacteristically accommodating.

On Tuesday, Lucy was on the road by eight-thirty, which turned out to be a very good thing. She made good time on the drive to Augusta, but her GPS completely failed her when she got to the office park where the state fire marshal's office was located. It was a maze of confusing roads and it took her some time before she located the public safety building, where the office was located. Once there, she encountered strict security and had to provide her credentials and allow her bag to be searched; only then was she allowed to pass through the metal detector.

It all seemed to be a lot of fuss about nothing. When she got to the press room she found only a handful of reporters had bothered to show up. The room was clearly set up for an important event: a large video screen stood behind a long table equipped with microphones, and chairs had been set out for at least fifty people. Lucy took a seat next to Bob Mayes, who was a stringer for the *Boston Globe*.

When state fire marshal Sam Carey took his seat, along with three or four others, he was obviously disappointed at the lack of interest. "This has been a remarkably successful investigation, and was conducted in record time," he announced. "I'm a big believer in giving credit where credit is due, and a good deal of credit goes to the Tinker's Cove Fire Department, which provided important evidence." He gave a nod to Buzz Bresnahan, the Tinker's Cove fire chief, who was seated at the end of the table.

Lucy caught Buzz's eye and gave him a little wave as she copied the quote in her long, narrow, spiral-bound reporter's notebook.

"I'm going to pass this over to Phil Simmons, the fire investigator who led the investigation into the fatal Tinker's Cove fire," Carey said, passing the mic to a large, heavy man with curly brown hair and a thick beard.

"Let me begin by saying this investigation was considerably simplified by the fact we knew the fire originated with an explosion. We have the incident records from the TCFD, which responded to a loud explosive blast at precisely oh-nine-one-six hours on November twenty-third. According to this report, the structure at Thirty-five Parallel Street was close to flashover point when the first engine arrived at oh-nine-twenty hours. This is consistent with observed test fire patterns in which a temperature of six hundred degrees was reached between one hundred seventy-three and two hundred fifty-six seconds."

Lucy did a quick computation, discovering that it only took a little more than four minutes for a fire to grow out of control.

"Response was hampered by the fact that the home owner was a hoarder and access to the home was blocked by falling debris. The fire was also fed by this debris, which included a large amount of newspaper. Responders had no choice but to allow the fire to burn and concentrated their efforts on protecting adjacent homes.

"I'll hand this over to Chief Bresnahan now, and he can give you his personal response to the situation."

Buzz Bresnahan was dressed in his official fire chief suit, the one he wore to all the funerals, and all that navy blue and gleaming brass made him look a lot more impressive than the plaid shirt and jeans he usually wore. He squared his shoulders and leaned forward to speak into the mic.

"The heat from the fire was already quite intense when we arrived and flashover occurred before we got any hoses operational. Access to the structure was blocked, but the initial explosion had blown out a couple of windows in the kitchen area, which allowed oxygen to feed the fire. This abnormally high fuel load along with the abundant oxygen made for a very hot fire. Added to this was the heavy load of hoarded materials on the second floor, which caused the second story to collapse." He paused. "I've been criticized for not taking a more aggressive approach to this fire but my first responsibility is to the firefighters and I was not about to endanger their lives. It was only a matter of minutes before that fire reached at least a thousand degrees and it would have been suicide for anyone to attempt to enter the structure."

Lucy wrote it down: *a thousand degrees*. She couldn't imagine such heat. Her oven went to five hundred degrees, tops. A thousand degrees would be twice as hot. No wonder the fire had been so destructive.

"I made the decision to let the fire burn itself out and then to do everything I could to recover what evidence we could for the state crime lab to analyze," he concluded.

"That brings us to the next stage of the investigation," Phil Simmons said. "Jim Cronin is with the Fire Debris Analysis Unit and he'll tell us what they were able to discover."

"People think most of the evidence is destroyed in a fire but that is not necessarily true," said Cronin, a tall, intense man whose hair was thinning. "We used two of our fire dogs, Blaze and Smoky. Blaze is trained to identify human remains and Smoky's specialty is accelerants. They were both successful. Blaze found a badly damaged body, which was identified by dental work as that of Jake Marlowe. Smoky indicated debris containing accelerant, and using chromatography we identified two sources: PETN, a nitroglycerin-style compound that we think created the initial explosion, and kerosene, most likely from a heater, which would explain the rapid ignition that took place."

"Now, as to the cause of death, I'm going to pass this over to Dr. Fred Singh, in the medical examiner's office."

Dr. Singh had a full head of black hair, thick glasses, and was wearing a white lab coat. "This was a very badly damaged body," he began. "I didn't have much to work with. I was able, however, to get a positive identification from the victim's dentist, who recognized bridgework that survived the fire more or less intact. Damage to remaining bone fragments indicate both hands were amputated by the blast. It was also possible to determine that there was considerable damage to the thorax, which leads to the conclusion that death was instantaneous due to the explosive blast, and not a result of the fire."

Amputation, bone fragments, not much to work with . . . the words rattled around in her head and she felt dizzy. *Death was instantaneous.* . . . That was a mercy, at least, but why would anyone intentionally and deliberately wish to inflict such a terrible fate on a fellow human being? It made her feel queasy, sick to her stomach, to imagine such evil.

"So this Marlowe was beyond saving, right?" she heard someone ask. It was Frank Harris, from the *Portland Press Herald,* seated just in front of her. She focused on the back of his neck, dotted with freckles, and the collar of his blue and green plaid shirt, and the nausea passed.

"Correct," Singh said. He looked around. "Any more questions?"

Lucy hoped not. She wanted to get out of there and

into the fresh air, but Bob Mayes raised his hand and got a nod. "So this explosion was the result of a package bomb, is that right?"

Sam Carey decided to answer that one. "Yes. The postal service was able to provide us with information that a package was delivered to the house shortly before the explosion, and PETN is consistent with that type of device. The postal worker who delivered the package remembered it because it was wrapped in festive paper, and had a *Do Not Open Till Christmas* label. He said it weighed about a pound, also consistent with the force of the explosion."

Lucy wasn't going to think about it, wasn't going to entertain the possibility that it could have been Wilf, instead of Marlowe, who was killed by the bomb. Not sweet, kind Wilf, who loved Phyllis and was loved back. Not for even one second. She was shaking her head to banish the thought when Bob Mayes followed up with a second question.

"So is there some sort of Ted Kaczynski guy out there, sending mail bombs?" he asked.

"I sure hope not," Carey said, "but only time will tell. I can tell you this: the state police, assisted by my department as well as the local Tinker's Cove PD, are vigorously investigating this crime."

Chapter Seven

On the drive back to Tinker's Cove Lucy found herself rehashing the press conference, despite herself. The details she'd learned were truly horrible. She hadn't really thought about the damage a mail bomb could do to a human body, and now she knew more than she wanted to know. Worst of all, however, was the notion that some insane person might at this very moment be busy building more mail bombs and disguising them as Christmas gifts. It really took the fun out of Christmas, she thought with a shudder, when you were afraid to open the packages that were such a feature of the holiday season. Even worse, she'd done most of her shopping this year on the Internet, which meant a steady stream of packages was already coming to the house.

It was almost lunchtime when she reached Tinker's Cove, so she took a detour through the McDonald's drive-through, but when she studied the menu she had another surge of nausea and ended up driving on without ordering. Phyllis and Ted were both out, so she quickly typed up the press conference story, skipping over the most gruesome details. The *Pennysaver* was a family newspaper, she rationalized, and she didn't want to give anybody nightmares. It was bad enough knowing she'd have trouble sleeping tonight herself.

She had finished the story and was sending it to Ted's file for editing when Phyllis arrived, carrying several large shopping bags with the Country Cousins logo.

"Christmas shopping?" Lucy asked.

"Yeah." Phyllis set down the bags and unbuttoned her coat. "Ted's at that conference today and I figured I might not get another chance to shop for Wilf. Togetherness is great—but I want his presents to be a surprise. I got him that fancy thermal underwear he's been talking about—and some snazzy pajamas."

"I'm all done, thanks to the Internet," Lucy said, wishing she could go home and take the dog for a walk, anything to clear her head and lift her mood, but that was out of the question so close to deadline. She needed to work on something that would catch her interest, so she decided to tackle the foreclosure story, and called Annie Kraus, who now worked part-time in the health department.

When she identified herself and explained the reason for her call, Annie was reluctant to talk. "I don't know, Lucy," she said. "I don't want everybody in town to know about my troubles."

"I don't have to use your name," Lucy said.

"People will know it's me," Annie objected.

"Well, if they already know, they might as well get the whole story," Lucy replied. "People need to know that low taxes come with a high price."

"That's a good one, Lucy," Annie said.

"Maybe a headline," Lucy said.

"Okay. Well, what happened to me and Larry is

pretty much the same thing that happened to a lot of people. We found a cute little house that was just perfect for us. It was the cheapest house in town, but even so it was priced quite high. They were eager to help us over at Downeast, however, and signed us up with an adjustable rate mortgage. It started out at a very low interest rate but then it jumped up after a few years. By that time prices were already falling, the mortgage was for more than the house was worth, but we were managing to make the payments. Just managing. Then my hours were cut and it didn't make any sense for us to sacrifice everything to keep the house. The stress was taking a toll on our relationship, Larry and I weren't really getting along, so we decided to separate and I went back home to live with my parents."

"What about Larry?" Lucy asked, thinking that losing his wife and his home could certainly make a fellow angry. That anger might have motivated him to send the mail bomb.

"Oh, he reenlisted in the coast guard. He's on a high-endurance cutter somewhere in the Caribbean, fighting the war against drugs." She paused. "He's got a leave coming up and I'm hoping we'll get back together."

"I hope it works out for you," Lucy said, thanking Annie and crossing Larry off her list of suspects, feeling rather ashamed of herself for suspecting a man who was serving his country.

The next town employee on her list was Nelson Macmillan, who was now a part-time natural resources officer. When she called him he was more than happy to chat; he said he had a lot of free time on his hands these days.

"It was an investment," he said. "I was caught up in

the real estate craze, and it seemed like a no-brainer. My 401(k) wasn't growing like I thought it should, certainly not like real estate, so I cashed out, took the penalty and tax hit, and put it all into a building lot. I had about seventy-five thousand and I financed another seventy-five and thought I'd retire a rich man when I got around to selling it." He chuckled ruefully. "It never occurred to me that I wouldn't be able to keep up the payments. I had seniority, terrific performance evaluations. What could go wrong?"

"The stock market took a dive, too," Lucy said. "Your 401(k) would've lost value, too."

"That's what I keep telling myself," Nelson said. "And I would've been okay, really, if I hadn't had my hours cut."

"So you must be pretty mad at the Finance Committee," Lucy suggested.

"They were faced with a tough situation, too. Tax revenues were down—what could they do? They had to balance the budget. I don't blame them."

Lucy wondered if he was really telling the truth. "You're very philosophical," she said.

"I don't know about that. Truth is, I'm better off than a lot of folks. I own my house free and clear, got enough for groceries and bills. I took a loss, sure, but it was a loss I could afford. The ones I feel sorry for are the folks who are losing their houses—they're the ones who are really hurting. Especially the ones with kids."

"You're right," Lucy said, putting a question mark next to his name. She suspected Nelson Macmillan might be a lot angrier than he was willing to admit.

One more call, she decided, and then she'd make herself a cup of tea. She dialed Frankie La Chance, her neighbor on Prudence Path who was a real estate agent. Frankie would be able to tell her how the foreclosures were affecting the local real estate market, as well as the increasingly tight rental market.

Frankie answered on the first ring, which rather took Lucy by surprise. "You must be sitting by the phone," she said.

"You know it," Frankie said. "Calls are few and far between and I don't want to miss one."

"That bad?" Lucy asked.

"It's the worst I've ever seen," Frankie said. "Houses that were going for five or six hundred thousand are on the market for two or three, and nobody's buying. Believe me, now's the time to invest. Prices have never been lower, but nobody's got any capital."

"What about rentals?" Lucy asked. "My daughter says rents are going up."

"Is Sara looking for a rental?" Frankie asked, quick to sense a possible opportunity. "I'd be happy to help her find one."

Lucy chuckled, thinking it wasn't very long ago that Frankie spurned rentals, saying they were too much trouble for a small commission. "She'd like to get a place of her own but she doesn't have any money," Lucy said.

"She's not alone, that's for sure," Frankie said. "And she's right—rents are going up a bit, because people have to live somewhere when they lose their homes." She paused. "Is this for the paper?"

"Uh, yeah," Lucy said. "I'm doing a story on foreclosures. Do you mind if I quote you?"

"Oh, no, I'm grateful. Just be sure to mention my company, La Chance and Raymond Real Estate."

"Will do," Lucy said. "Thanks for your time." She added her notes from the call to her developing story, then got up to fill the kettle.

"Put in enough for two," Phyllis said. "I brought in some cocoa mix. With mini marshmallows."

"I better stick to tea," Lucy said, still not trusting her tummy. She unwrapped a tea bag and dropped it in her cup, tore open a packet of cocoa mix, which she poured into Phyllis's mug, then went over to the window to check the sky. Snow had been predicted but you wouldn't know it from the bright blue, cloudless sky. Of course, New England was known for rapid weather changes. If you didn't like the weather, people said, just wait a few minutes. Nevertheless, it seemed a shame to be stuck inside on such a fine day. She'd rather be out in the woods behind her house with Libby, cutting greens to decorate the house and searching for the perfect balsam Christmas tree.

The kettle whistled and Lucy filled the mugs; she was just giving Phyllis her cocoa when the police scanner went off. Lucy didn't recognize the code but she knew the address.

Once again it was Downeast Mortgage.

Abandoning her tea, she grabbed her jacket and headed out the door. The fire trucks were already racing down Main Street, and she followed on foot, figuring the car would only be an encumbrance.

She was out of breath when she joined the small crowd of bystanders that Barney Culpepper was urging to step back. The reason was clear: a gaily wrapped package with a *Do Not Open Till Christmas* label was lying on the sidewalk in front of the Downeast Mortgage office. She stared at it, eyes wide with terror, aware of the terrible damage it could inflict if it was what it seemed to be: a second bomb.

"We don't want a tragedy," he was saying, as a couple of firemen began unrolling a bright yellow *Do Not Cross* tape, creating a spacious perimeter around the package and moving the bystanders some distance down the street. "You don't want to be anywhere near that thing if it goes off."

"How long before the bomb squad gets here?" Lucy asked. The details she'd learned that morning about the bomb that blew up Marlowe's house were all too fresh in her mind and she eyed the package warily.

"Any time now. Lucky for us they were at a training session in Knoxport."

Lucy studied the package, a rectangular shape wrapped in red and green Christmas paper. "How'd it get here? It doesn't look like it was mailed."

"It wasn't," Barney said. "Elsie found it hanging from the knob in a plastic grocery bag—you know how people do, when the door is locked."

Lucy knew. She'd often done the same thing, leaving a requested book or returning a potluck dish, when nobody answered the door. "Do you really think it's a bomb?" she asked. "The bomb that killed Marlowe was sent in the mail."

"We're not taking any chances," Barney said, as the bomb team's special van arrived with a containment trailer in tow. The team, which consisted of four extremely fit-looking young men in blue uniforms and one German shepherd dog, assembled outside the vehicle. Soon one member was dressed in bulky protective padding, and the dog was also togged out in a flak jacket.

Lucy snapped photos as the dog and its handler cautiously approached the suspect package.

It was a tense moment and everyone who was watching seemed to be holding their breath. When the dog froze, keeping his eyes fixed on the package, there was a general inhalation followed by a burst of panicked chatter. "It's the real thing," said one woman. "Oh my God," said another, white-faced with tension.

Then the dog and its handler withdrew to the van while another bomb squad member conferred with fire chief Buzz Bresnahan. Moments later the crew opened one of the van's doors and pulled out a metal ramp, allowing a remote-controlled robot to descend. All eyes were on the robot, watching as it approached the package.

Lucy worked her way through the crowd until she was beside Buzz. "That's quite a gadget," she said.

"They call it Andros," he said. "They got it with Homeland Security money. It's got an extendable arm and four video cameras."

Lucy studied the mechanical marvel, which ran on four wheels, had one arm, and a video camera for a head. "It looks like something a kid could make out of Legos," she said.

"No way. This is highly sophisticated machinery. It was just luck that the squad was so close today," Buzz said. "Otherwise we'd have had to wait for them to make the trip from Bangor."

"Pretty lucky." Lucy noticed Ben Scribner and Elsie, standing in a tight group along with other evacuees from nearby businesses. They were all wearing worried expressions and generally looking quite miserable in the cold. Only a few had thought to grab coats or jackets.

Scribner was more warmly dressed than most, in a Harris tweed jacket, but he was visibly shivering. Lucy wondered if he was reacting to the chilly weather or actually quaking with fear. Elsie, who seemed capable of handling any challenge, was wearing a fur-trimmed parka and had pulled the hood up so that it covered her face. Maybe she was protecting her complexion from the cold, Lucy thought. Or maybe she wanted to hide her fear? Or perhaps she was concealing a different emotion?

Lucy's attention was diverted by the robot, which was advancing toward the package, moving at a stately pace and emitting a humming noise. When it was within a few feet it stopped and the arm was maneuvered so that it picked up the package. Then Andros rolled backward along the sidewalk until it reached the containment trailer, where the suspect package was deposited. The trailer was sealed, Andros returned to its compartment, and the bomb squad members, including the dog, returned to their van and drove off, leaving the yellow tape fluttering around an empty sidewalk.

Lucy got busy, requesting comments from a few of the bystanders. Dora Fraser, from the nearby fudge shop, was full of praise for the bomb team. "If that thing had gone off," she said, "my store would've been blown to kingdom come." Cliff Sandstrom, who worked at the liquor store across the street, shared his concern about a second package bomb. "I hope this isn't the work of some maniac," he said, furrowing his brow.

Lucy also wanted to get a reaction from Ben Scribner, but there was no sign of him on the street and when she tried the office door she discovered it was locked. She knocked, but nobody answered. Pulling out her cell phone, she called, but her call went to voice mail. She left a message, then walked back to the office, reviewing the photos in her digital camera on the way.

Ted was going to love them, she decided, especially the one with the dog. The handsome German shepherd was clearly focused on the package one hundred percent, performing the life-saving work he was trained to do. She thought of her own lab, Libby, who was really only interested in her next meal. If only she could be more like this heroic bomb-sniffing dog. She made a mental note to call the bomb team to get their names, including the dog's. Especially the dog's.

When Lucy got back to the *Pennysaver* office, however, she discovered she didn't need to make the call after all. Buzz Bresnahan had already e-mailed her a press release about the entire incident, with numerous attachments containing information about the bomb team, including the fact that the dog's name was Boomer. She sent a quick reply thanking him, aware that in the current financial climate every Tinker's Cove department head had to become a public relations expert. Buzz was defending his department from budget cuts, and he made it very clear in his press release that the bomb squad was funded by the state, assisted by the federal Department of Homeland Security.

Lucy made sure she included that information in the story, but put it at the end, leading with the human interest angle, the dog, Boomer. She was just winding up the story and thinking about heading home when Ted announced he had received an e-mail from the bomb squad.

Recalling Boomer's immediate response to the suspicious package, she wasn't entirely surprised to learn that it was discovered to be completely innocent of any explosives. It contained an assortment of sausages sent to Scribner from his insurance agent.

"It came prewrapped," said Bill Swift, of Swift and Chase, when she called him for a reaction. "I wanted to express my appreciation to my best customers. I never thought—I mean—I'm so sorry."

Ending that call, Lucy decided to follow up with the bomb squad after all. "What did you do with the sausage?" she asked.

"Oh, we ate it," came the reply, "but we gave most of it to Boomer. That dog really loves sausage."

Chapter Eight

Harriet Sigafoo, the organist, pulled out all the stops for the final hymn, "Just a Closer Walk with Thee," and the mourners gathered for Jake Marlowe's funeral on Friday morning were clearly eager to get moving as soon as they sang that last amen. Jake Marlowe hadn't been very popular in his life and Lucy suspected quite a few people had come simply to make sure the old miser was really and truly dead. Now that they had been assured that this was indeed the case, they were eager to see what was being offered in the collation the minister had invited everyone to partake of in the Fellowship Hall.

As she waited for her pew to empty, Lucy thought of the lines of the hymn: "When my feeble life is o'er / Time for me will be no more. / Guide me gently, safely o'er / To Thy kingdom shore, to Thy shore." Jake Marlowe had run out of time rather sooner than he'd expected, and Lucy wondered if he would have made some different choices if he'd known his end was so close. Perhaps he would have forgiven some debtors, hoping that his own sinful debts would be forgiven. Or perhaps not, she thought, remembering Elsie's warning about moral hazard. Perhaps he thought he was the righteous one and the pearly gates would open wide for him.

Personally, Lucy doubted it. At the very least she expected St. Peter would consign him to a lengthy spell in purgatory, to consider his moral lapses. Jesus said it was easier for a camel to get through the eye of a needle than for a rich man to enter heaven, and Lucy thought that was probably true in Jake Marlowe's case. She assumed exceptions would be made for rich people who shared their wealth and tried to make the world a better place, people like Bono and Bill Gates. Jake Marlowe hadn't done that. In truth, his single-minded pursuit of wealth had caused a great deal of misery.

Joining the line of people who were filing into the Fellowship Hall, Lucy thought she caught a tantalizing whiff of Fern's Famous Swedish meatballs. Not what she expected, she thought, recalling Phyllis's prediction of tea punch and lemon cookies. But first, she had to negotiate the reception line.

"I'm terribly sorry for your loss," she murmured to Ben Scribner. He seemed quite subdued, she thought, murmuring a barely audible thank you. She suspected he was still quite shaken by the incident with the suspicious package; even though it turned out to be completely harmless it must have been a terrifying experience. He passed her along to his niece, Florence, who greeted her warmly and introduced her to Virginia Irving, Marlowe's ex-wife.

Lucy caught her jaw before it dropped; she never would have guessed that Marlowe was once married, and certainly not to someone as attractive as Virginia.

She was an energetic fifty or so, with a fashionable short hairdo. Her skin glowed, her eyes were bright, and any gray hairs were covered with an auburn rinse. She was wearing a subdued greenish gray dress, but instead of the usual black pumps was sporting a pair of very fashionable high-heeled ankle boots.

"Lucy and I have parts in *A Christmas Carol*," Florence was saying. "I hope you'll come to the show."

"I'd love to," Virginia said with a warm smile. "It's my favorite Christmas story."

"Mine, too," Lucy said, moving along to check out the buffet table.

"Quite a spread," Marge Culpepper said, getting in line beside her. "I heard that the ex-wife is paying for it."

Lucy surveyed the chafing dishes filled with Swedish meatballs, flounder roll-ups with crab stuffing, chicken Kiev, and beef Stroganoff and concluded Marge was right. The long table seemed to go on and on, offering potatoes au gratin, rice pilaf, buttery noodles, mixed vegetables, a huge bowl of salad, rolls with butter, and then there was a separate dessert table with tea and coffee. "That must be the case," she said. "Ben Scribner would never spend the money for something this lavish."

"You're right about that. Mrs. Irving is the founder of this feast and she's a sweetie," Dora Fraser said, spooning a healthy serving of meatballs onto Lucy's plate. "I don't know what she ever saw in that miserable old codger, but it's thanks to her that we're going to have Christmas after all. Believe me, just last week I was studying my checkbook and figuring we could have either prime rib for Christmas dinner or presents, but not both."

"If Jake Marlowe knew about this he'd be spinning in his grave like a top," Marge said. "I hope they've got him down a good six feet."

"Considering the state of his body, I guess he'd be more like a dust devil," Dora said.

"You're terrible, Dora," Lucy said, adding salad to her plate.

"But you know she's right," Marge said, bursting into giggles.

Looking around, Lucy had to admit there were no sad faces at Jake Marlowe's funeral. She and Marge seated themselves at a table set for four and were soon joined by Pam and Sue. They were a merry group, chatting about their holiday plans. Lucy resisted the temptation to have a second helping of those famous meatballs, and decided to forgo the tempting desserts in favor of a cup of tea. She was just returning to the table when she encountered Virginia and Florence.

"Is everything all right?" Virginia asked. "Is there enough food?"

"Plenty of food and everything is lovely," Lucy said, "and to be honest, quite unexpected. You must have been very fond of Jake Marlowe."

"I was once, many years ago, but we grew apart," Virginia said. "He changed—that's why our marriage ended. But now that he's gone, I want to remember the man he used to be." She gave a sad smile. "My therapist would say it's wishful thinking."

"That's an interesting view," Lucy said, turning to Florence. "How is your uncle taking the loss? And on top of losing his partner, there was the bomb scare. . . ."

"He won't admit it, he's keeping a stiff upper lip, but he's really upset. Losing Jake was like losing part of himself, his right hand or something. They've been partners for thirty-odd years," Florence said. "And now the idea that somebody out there wanted to do Jake harm—that's really shaken him. He feels very vulnerable and that doesn't fit in with his world view. He's the one who's supposed to be in charge."

"It must be quite upsetting," Lucy said, privately thinking it was high time the old cheapskate got a reality check. "Has he had any more panic attacks?"

"No. Doc Ryder gave him some antianxiety medication but I'm not convinced he's taking it." She indicated her uncle, who was sitting by himself in a corner. "As a matter of fact, I think I better go and cheer him up."

"I'll come, too," Virginia said. "It was nice talking to you, Lucy."

Lucy sipped her tea, watching them cross the room. Noticing a photo collage depicting Jake Marlowe's life, she decided to take a look at it. She was curious about him, wondering why he'd become such a miserly hermit, and perhaps the photos would offer an explanation.

The first thing Lucy noticed was that someone had gone to a great deal of trouble to create the display, and she assumed that person was Virginia. The photos were beautifully mounted, in chronological sequence, and had captions written in a lovely calligraphic hand. The photo essay began with a graying photo of an infant tightly grasping a silver rattle, which must have been taken when Jake was only a few months old. That was followed with five or six snapshots, clearly taken together, of a chubby towheaded toddler pulling a little wooden wagon.

Studying the photos, Lucy wondered why Virginia had kept them. She was now Mrs. Irving, so she must have remarried. Once a divorce was final, she imagined most women were eager to get on with their lives and got rid of reminders of their failed marriage, even throwing away their wedding rings. Or maybe that was just in the movies, she thought, examining the pictures that documented Jake's progress through elementary school, prep school (*St. Paul's* read the flowing script), and college (Dartmouth).

At St. Paul's he was pictured arm in arm with three other teens, and at Dartmouth he seemed to be quite the life of the party, caught by the camera in company with numerous other glowing youths. The glow, Lucy suspected, came from plenty of alcohol.

But why had Jake changed from the sociable fellow he had been in his youth to the miser he became in later life? It was hard to believe the young man pictured at his first job with longish, curly hair, wearing a once fashionable suit with bell bottom pants, was the same person who lived in that ramshackle house stuffed with old newspapers. There was a clue, perhaps, in the fact that his first job was with a venture capital firm and he was smiling broadly and proudly displaying a fan of hundred-dollar bills in his hand.

There were only a few more photos in the display, and none from Marlowe's later life, confirming Virginia's confession that they had grown apart. Hearing her voice, Lucy looked for a way to get a bit closer to the corner where Virginia and Ben Scribner were sitting. Noticing the memory book set out on a nearby table, she bent over it and began turning the pages.

"Remember when you two met at Fitzhugh Capital?" Virginia was saying. "Old Fitz was a wonderful boss, wasn't he? Remember those fabulous dinners at Locke-

Ober's? That Christmas party at the Ritz? The champagne corks were going off like popcorn!" She shook her head, her voice rueful. "When did it all start to go wrong?"

Ben shrugged and shook his head. "Jake was a good partner. I couldn't have asked for better. I'd trust him with my last penny."

"You know," Virginia said, "when I asked for a divorce it was because I thought he was having an affair with another woman, but it wasn't a woman at all. It was money. He fell in love with money."

"He was a good businessman," Ben said. "Nothing wrong with that."

"Oh but there is," Virginia said, placing her hand on Ben's. "There's more to life than business, and I'm afraid you're making the same mistake Jake did. He fell in love with money and it seems you've fallen into that trap, too."

"Nonsense!" Ben said, shaking off her hand and rising unsteadily to his feet. "You're being ridiculous." He waved his hand. "Look at all this! A waste of money!"

Virginia's face was white, and she bit her lip. "No, Ben, not a waste. The waste was Jake's life, hiding himself away in that big old house."

Ben glared at her, but all he was able to come up with in response was a big "Hmph!"

Lucy picked up the pen and wrote her name in the memory book, and when she finished she saw that both Virginia and Ben had left their seats. They weren't the only ones; the room was definitely emptying. Lucy plucked a single cookie from the dessert table and nibbled it, making her way to the coatrack. She was there, buttoning her coat, when Ike Stoughton joined her.

"I didn't expect such a good turnout," he said.

"Funerals are always popular in Tinker's Cove," Lucy said, drawing on long experience.

"Maybe so," Ike admitted. "But I suspect a lot of people wanted to make sure the old bastard was really dead—and the free meal was a bonus."

"There's that, too," Lucy replied, but she was talking to Ike's back. He'd turned, spotting Ben Scribner, and had crossed the small vestibule to approach him, actually cornering him. Ben was looking uncomfortable, but Lucy couldn't hear what Ike was saying, although he did appear to be asking for a favor of some kind. Whatever it was, Scribner wasn't pleased. He was shaking his head and trying to get around Ike.

Suddenly Ike's voice rose. "I tell you, I just need a bit more time. I can pay you next month."

"This is not the place to discuss business," Scribner snarled, glaring at him. "Call my office and make an appointment."

"I'll do that," Ike said. Realizing he was drawing attention to himself, he stepped aside, and Scribner scurried to the coatrack in a sideways move that reminded Lucy of a frightened crab running for cover. Once he'd pulled on his overcoat, he seemed to regain his usual arrogant attitude.

"I don't imagine it will make any difference," Scribner said, pulling his leather gloves from his coat pocket and slapping them against his hand. "A contract is a contract." Then Elsie, his secretary, joined him and the two left the hall, walking in the direction of the Downeast office.

"I bet they're going back to work," Ike said. "He

wouldn't even close the business for one day in honor of his partner."

"Oh, that's the last thing Jake Marlowe would have wanted," Lucy said. "He'd expect them to carry on with business as usual."

Ike snorted in disgust. "Unbelievable," he said, shrugging into his bulky down jacket and holding the door for Lucy. They parted when the path met the sidewalk and she headed back to the office, enjoying the opportunity to clear her head in the crisp, cold air.

As she began the short, four-block walk along Main Street to the *Pennysaver* office, Lucy thought that Ike Stoughton was absolutely the last person she would expect to have financial problems. He had a successful surveying business and was known as the man to go to if you had a problem with a property title. Of course, the recession had taken a toll on business, especially real estate. Nevertheless, even foreclosures required accurate surveying, which should have provided at least some work for him.

Probably, she admitted, nothing like what he was doing before the recession, when real estate was booming. These days everybody, it seemed, was making do with less and Ike Stoughton was no exception. Unfortunately for him, Lucy knew, he had high expenses for his daughter, Abby, who had suffered a mental breakdown following the death of her mother.

Lucy paused at a corner, waiting for a car to pass, then crossed the street. When your income dropped you could cut back on some things, but not medical care, especially when your daughter was suicidal. Ike was committed to Abby, and he wanted the best for her, but that didn't come cheap. It was the sort of thing that could make for a motive, Lucy thought. Ike wasn't one to knuckle under to anyone and he might be just angry enough to do something foolish. If he sent the bomb, Lucy was sure he had only meant to scare Jake Marlowe and his partner, Ben Scribner—he wouldn't have meant to kill anybody. Just try telling that to a jury!

When Lucy reached the corner of Main and Sea streets the cackle of an amplified voice caught her attention. Glancing down the hill in the direction of the cove, she noticed a crowd gathered in front of Seamen's Bank and decided to see what it was all about. As she drew closer she recognized the speaker as Seth Lesinski, who was leading Winchester College students in another protest demonstration.

"We all know what the stock market bubble did to workers' savings, don't we?" he asked rhetorically. "It wiped out their retirement savings."

The kids in the crowd all voiced agreement.

"And we know what the housing bubble did to families, don't we? It made them homeless."

Lucy studied the faces of the demonstrators. Most were young, but there were a few older people, too. She recognized several professors from the college, and some of the kids, too, who were Sara's friends. They were clustered together, at Seth Lesinski's feet, and several girls were gazing at him raptly, hanging on every word he uttered. One of them, she realized, was Sara. And Sara, she happened to know, was supposed to be in class. She began worming her way through the crowd, intending to give her daughter a piece of her mind.

"Well, the next bubble is student debt and it's crippling the economy," Lesinski proclaimed. "Student debt is now greater than all the consumer debt combined.

Not a problem, you think. What did they tell you and me? That student debt is okay because you'll be able to get a good job and pay it back. Sounds good, doesn't it, if you can get a job. But that's a big *if*, with real unemployment at eighteen percent. So what's going to happen when you and I can't pay back our loans? It's the next big bust and our generation is going to start out bankrupt!"

Now Lucy was behind her daughter and she tapped her on the shoulder. Startled, Sara whirled around. "Mom! What are you doing here?"

"That's what I want to know!" Lucy exclaimed. "What are *you* doing here when you ought to be in class?"

"Mom, what does it matter? We're all gonna be broke. Missing a class or two isn't going to make a bit of difference. It's not like I'm going to be able to get a job, anyway. I might as well give up now, instead of getting thousands of dollars deeper in debt."

Lucy couldn't believe what she was hearing; it went against everything she'd taught her children. Her kids had to go to college. It was the surest way to a successful career. She'd been so disappointed when Toby dropped out, and so pleased when he'd decided to go back to school and get his degree. There had been times when her oldest daughter, Elizabeth, also wanted to drop out, but Lucy had coaxed and cajoled and convinced her to stick with her studies. She'd graduated from Chamberlain College in Boston with honors and was now in the Cavendish Hotel chain's executive training program.

"Don't be crazy!" she said, yelling over the noise of the crowd. "Look at Elizabeth. She's got a great job."

"Seamen's Bank is ripping you off!" Seth proclaimed, and a number of the kids in the crowd yelled out in agreement. "They're getting rich and you're getting poor!"

"Come on, Sara," Lucy urged. "Let's get out of here."

Sara shook her head. "No, Mom. I'm staying. This is important to me."

Flummoxed, Lucy sucked her teeth. There wasn't anything she could do. She couldn't grab her daughter by the hair and drag her off to class. The only thing she could do was threaten her. "I'm going to tell your father," she said, through a clenched jaw. "Don't think I won't!"

Sara rolled her eyes, then turned her attention to the leader of the protest. "We demand amnesty!" Seth Lesinski yelled, raising his arm and unleashing a wave of shouts. "Amnesty! Amnesty! We demand amnesty!"

Lucy's emotions were in turmoil and her head was ringing from the noise. It was time for her to leave. She slipped through the crowd and began climbing the hill, shaking her head. What was she going to do about Sara? Even worse, what if she was right? Maybe it was crazy to spend tens of thousands of dollars to get her a bachelor's degree when she could spend a few months learning medical billing or massage therapy and have a salable skill. Maybe she should join the coast guard, thought Lucy, recalling a TV commercial and thinking of Annie Kraus's husband.

"Careful!" a voice warned, and Lucy lifted her head, realizing she was about to walk into a lamppost. Embarrassed, she turned and recognized Phil Watkins, the assistant building inspector. He was a friendly guy and they always exchanged pleasantries when she stopped by town hall.

"Thanks," she said with a rueful smile. "I was distracted, wasn't paying attention."

"Happens to all of us," he said, shrugging. "Did I see Sara down there?"

"Oh, yes," Lucy said. "She's become a social activist." She paused. "Were you demonstrating or watching?"

"Demonstrating," Phil said. "Face it, since they cut my hours I've got plenty of time on my hands—and plenty of student loans. If it wasn't for the student loan payments I wouldn't have lost my house." He winced. "Or maybe not. Maybe I'm just kidding myself, but they sure didn't help."

"That house was a labor of love, wasn't it?" Lucy asked. She knew Phil had built his LEED-certified green home himself, banging in every nail.

"Yeah." He nodded. "It's the only LEED house in town. It's energy efficient, built with recycled and sustainable materials."

Lucy knew that; she'd written a story about the project, which was not only kind to the environment but also beautiful and livable. "It's a shame you couldn't work something out with Downeast Mortgage."

Phil scowled. "You know what really sticks in my craw? It's the way Scribner made out like a bandit. That house is worth plenty, even in this depressed market. It's entirely green and a lot of folks, especially rich liberal types, the Prius crowd, are willing to pay for that. I did the work, I had the vision to make it happen, and Scribner's going to make a lot of money off my vision and hard work."

"That's the way it is," Lucy said, with a rueful smile. "The rich get richer and the poor get poorer."

"You said it! I heard that bastard's already sold Macmillan's lot for a fast food restaurant. . . ."

This was news to Lucy. "You mean that building lot of Nelson's?"

"Yeah. Turns out the state is rerouting part of Route 1 and that scrappy bit of pasture has suddenly become prime real estate. Once again, Scribner's going to make a killing." The driver of a green pickup truck honked and Phil looked up, recognizing a friend. He raised his arm in a wave and the truck pulled to the side of the street. "Well, nice talking to you, Lucy. Take care."

Then he hopped into the truck, joining his friend, and the two drove off together. The demonstration was still going strong, so Lucy pulled her camera out of her bag and snapped a few photos before heading back to the office. As she walked, she thought about what Phil Watkins had told her. Downeast Mortgage was certainly profiting from the recession, making a fortune off other people's misfortunes. That wasn't a crime, but that didn't mean it was right. It was no wonder there was a lot of bad feeling toward the company, and its principals, Marlowe and Scribner.

The one person she thought ought to be angry, Nelson Macmillan, had seemed quite philosophical about his loss. Here he'd bought a piece of property that had increased dramatically in value, but he hadn't been able to keep up the payments and he'd lost it. Why wasn't he angry? He stood to make a fortune, if only he'd been able to keep it. And then it hit her. Of course. As the natural resources officer, he would have had inside knowledge of the planned rerouting. His office would have been consulted as a matter of course, to make sure no protected wetlands or endangered species were involved. He'd had inside knowledge that he'd used to buy the neglected acreage, anticipating how it would increase in value.

It was no wonder he seemed so untroubled about his loss. He probably figured it was no more than he deserved, considering how he'd bent the rules in the first place. Or maybe, she thought, he was simply pretending not to be upset. Maybe he was hiding a deep anger, which he'd held close while he plotted his revenge.

Chapter Nine

Phyllis and Ted hadn't returned from the funeral when Lucy got to the office and she figured she knew what was keeping them. Phyllis was probably still gabbing with her friends from the knitting circle and Ted might well be taking advantage of a state senator's appearance at the funeral to discuss some upcoming legislative matters. Considering the senator's reputation, that discussion would most likely be continued in the Irish pub down by the cove and would probably take the rest of the afternoon.

It didn't matter. They weren't needed at the moment. The paper came out on Thursday morning and, except for a few callers with complaints, Friday afternoons were generally quiet. It was too early to start on next week's news cycle, so Lucy usually went through the press releases, looking for story ideas. Phyllis filed the notices by date in a bulky accordion file as they arrived, so Lucy took the file over to her desk and booted up her computer. While she waited for the ancient PC's clicks and grinds to subside, she checked her phone messages, discovering that the postmaster had called, informing Lucy that she would be in her office until 1:30 p.m.

According to the antique clock on the wall it was only twenty-five past, so Lucy quickly made the call. Sheila Finlay wasn't pleased at her timing.

"I was just leaving . . ." she grumbled.

"This won't take long," Lucy promised.

"Oh, all right," Sheila consented, sounding as if she thought she was doing Lucy a big favor.

Of course, the shoe was actually on the other foot: it was Lucy who was doing Sheila a favor. Publicizing the effect of the proposed cuts might well prompt public outcry, which could save the postal workers' jobs.

"What do these cuts mean for Tinker's Cove?" Lucy asked.

"The mail will come a day or two later, I guess," Sheila said. "They're closing the nearest distribution center, so the mail will take longer."

"What about jobs?" Lucy asked.

"Well, we'll lose some, I suppose." She paused. "I'm not at liberty—"

"Can you give me a percentage?" Lucy coaxed.

"I don't think so."

"I've heard some of the smaller post offices will be closed. Is there any danger that we'll lose our post office?" As in most small towns, the Tinker's Cove post office was an important gathering place where people caught up with their neighbors.

"Anything could happen," Sheila said.

Lucy felt like banging her head on the desk. "Do you think it will?" she persisted.

"I don't know." There was a long pause. "I have to go now."

Lucy still had a long list of questions she wanted to ask. "Before you go, what can you tell me about the package bomb . . . ?"

"I don't have anything to say about that."

"Well, thanks for your help," Lucy said, thinking that Sheila hadn't actually been any help at all. Maybe Ted got something from the state senator. Maybe she should call their congressional representative. Maybe she should just write up the inch or two she got from the postmaster and move on to something else.

She began leafing through the press releases, discovering that this Christmas season was going to be much like the last. Every church in the county was holding a Christmas bazaar, the ballet schools were all presenting *The Nutcracker,* and the Historical Society was holding a cookie sale and open house at the Ezekiel Hallett House. And, of course, the Community Players were presenting *A Christmas Carol.* Perhaps there was a story there, if she could come up with a new angle that would convince Ted.

She jotted down an idea or two, then ran out of steam. It was really quite chilly in the office and she was thinking about putting up the heat and debating whether it was worth risking a scolding from Ted, when and if he ever showed up. Maybe she should just make herself a cup of tea and put her coat back on. Maybe she should just get out of there, she decided, shoving her chair back under her desk. She still needed a few more interviews for the foreclosure story and a phone call wasn't nearly as informative as a face-to-face encounter.

Stepping outside, she discovered the sun had disappeared behind clouds and a brisk breeze was blowing off the cove, but Lucy didn't mind. She enjoyed being on the move, working on a story, and she hadn't spoken to Harry Crawford yet. She liked the harbormaster; most everybody did. He was pleasant and affable and generally helpful, unlike some public employees she could mention. He took his job seriously, aware of the dangers faced by those who ventured out to sea. It was one thing to take a pleasant sail on a warm summer day and quite another to chug out past Quissett Point on a dark, cold winter morning to check lobster traps, and Harry did everything he could to make sure that those who went out came back safely to shore.

Nevertheless, she had to admit that Harry had a heck of a motive for killing Jake Marlowe. His family had owned their oceanfront farm for more than two hundred years, raising sheep on the rocky pastures that sloped down to the cove. Now, Downeast Mortgage was selling off that two hundred and twenty acres in a foreclosure auction scheduled a few days after Christmas.

She'd felt sick herself when she saw the ad copy, and it wasn't even her land, so she could imagine how Harry and the other members of his family felt about losing the property. They might well have wanted to send a message, and Harry certainly had the skill to build a bomb. As a farmer and harbormaster he had developed the expertise to keep engines and other equipment working, and knew all about electric circuits. As for explosives, well, that information was all over the Internet.

But knowing Harry as she did, Lucy doubted he would have intended to kill Jake Marlowe. If he had sent the bomb, it would have been a desperate measure designed to frighten Jake, not take his life with a huge explosion and deadly fire.

Reaching Sea Street, Lucy was relieved to see that the demonstration in front of Seamen's Bank was over and the crowd was gone. The steep road that led down to the cove and the town's harbor was clear, only a few cars and trucks parked along the curb. Lucy paused at the top of the hill for a moment, taking in the view she loved from here. The cove hadn't iced over yet and a few lobster boats bobbed at anchor on the blue water. Others had already been taken out and put in storage, shrouded in shiny white shrink wrap and set on jacks in the parking lot.

There was very little activity today, no clanks and hammering, no buzz of engines. Only a little column of smoke rose from the Irish pub, where a cheerful, welcoming fire was kept burning all winter.

Lucy sniffed the pleasant scent of wood smoke as she made her way through the parking lot to the harbormaster's shed. The shed was about the size of a tollbooth, with windows on all sides. It was also empty, closed tight, with a notice on the door announcing the new, reduced hours.

Of course, she thought, feeling rather stupid. She knew Harry's hours had been cut and she should have checked the new schedule on the town's official website before she trudged all the way down here. She was turning to go when somebody called her voice and, shading her eyes with her hand, she noticed Gabe Franco at the fuel dock, pumping gas into his lobster boat.

"Hi, Gabe," she yelled back. "Howzit going?" Gabe's face was deeply tanned, even in winter, and he was wearing yellow oilskin overalls.

"Okay," he said. "Were you looking for Harry?"

"Yeah."

"Well, you know his hours were cut."

"It slipped my mind," Lucy admitted.

"Kind o' crazy, if you ask me. We're having the mildest winter in years and plenty of guys are still lobstering. And there's the oyster farm—they're out there nearly every day, harvesting. There's a big demand this time of year. But I guess they just don't understand at town hall about us folks down here at the harbor." He cocked his head toward Main Street. "There isn't anybody on that Finance Committee that makes a living working the water, not one."

Lucy knew he was right. Pam taught yoga part time, Frankie La Chance was a real estate broker, Jerry Taubert owned an insurance agency, and Gene Hawthorne was an innkeeper. The working people, those who actually worked with their hands, didn't have a representative. "You're right," she said. "Maybe you should offer yourself now that there's a vacancy."

"Not me," Gabe said, glancing at the sky and waving his arm at the wide open space all around him. "I couldn't take being stuck indoors at some meeting when there's all this out here."

"I think you're on to something," Lucy said, with a smile. She gave him a wave and headed back up the hill, listening to the wild calls of the herring gulls wheeling high overhead.

As she climbed up the steep incline she thought about Jake Marlowe's impact on the town, deciding it was extremely negative. Not only had he cut town employees' hours and benefits, reducing their income, but that lost income had hurt local businesses. The cuts also meant reduced services, which working people like Gabe and the other fishermen counted on. Even Bill, she remembered, had been complaining about how long waits for building inspectors were slowing his progress. And that was before you even took the foreclosures into account.

The foreclosures were the greatest source of discontent, however, and the likeliest motive for the package bomb. Phil Watkins, for example, was angry about losing his LEED-certified home and was quite outspoken about it. She wasn't sure if he was angriest about losing the house, or the fact that Downeast Mortgage was profiting handsomely from the foreclosure. Probably both, equally, she decided.

Then there was Nelson Macmillan, who had lost the opportunity of a lifetime. It wasn't every day that a scrappy piece of land littered with cast-off junk became the perfect spot for a fast-food restaurant, and he'd have made a bundle if he'd been able to hold on to it. But now Downeast Mortgage was collecting that bundle and Nelson had lost his retirement savings and was looking at a ruined credit rating. It was enough to make anyone think seriously about taking revenge.

She thought of Ike Stoughton, a proud man who'd humbled himself to beg Ben Scribner for a little more time to pay back his loan. Scribner hadn't been open to the idea; he'd been his usual high-and-mighty self. But Ike was only asking for a bit of time—there was no doubt that he would pay back whatever he borrowed. Everybody was feeling the squeeze, everybody was coping with payments that dribbled in slowly, or partial payments that came with promises to pay the rest "when I can." Lucy had seen the scribbled notes piling up on Bill's desk, IOUs for work he'd done in the last few months.

Bill wasn't taking those chits to small claims court, nor was he asking for liens on his debtors' income or property. Nobody was, except for the big national banks and Downeast Mortgage. Lucy had seen Dot Kirwan at the IGA wave away the offer of a postdated check, telling a cash-strapped customer to pay when he could. And she'd seen Phil Crawford, Harry's uncle, do the same thing at the Quik-Stop, when a young mother with two little kids strapped into her SUV didn't have quite enough cash to pay for her fill-up.

What difference would it make to Ben Scribner, she wondered, if he worked out new deals with mortgage holders instead of heading straight to court? She thought of Harry Crawford's family farm, going on the block. What good did it do? The Crawfords were losing a source of income, and perhaps more important, family pride. And for what? Ben Scribner certainly didn't need any more money—he had plenty.

Reaching the top of the hill and turning onto Main Street, she noticed a new sign had gone up. The Curl 'n' Cut beauty salon was now for sale, "price negotiable."

Well, thought Lucy, she hoped all these foreclosures were making Ben Scribner happy, since they were certainly causing a lot of misery for everyone else. And then it occurred to her that, of all the people in town, it was Ben Scribner who stood to profit most from his partner's death. Did Ben Scribner send that package bomb to Jake Marlowe? Lucy pressed her lips together, grimly. She wouldn't doubt it, not for a minute.

Chapter Ten

The sky was already darkening when she got to her car, the short winter afternoon almost over before it began. She decided to head home and grab a few minutes for herself, perhaps stretch out on the family room couch with a magazine. She had another rehearsal tonight and had to admit these late evenings were taking a toll. Ordinarily, she'd be joining the rest of the family at the town's annual carol sing, which was scheduled to take place that evening, but she figured the show had to go on, which meant she'd miss it this year.

She was almost home, approaching the corner of Bumps River Road, when she heard a siren. She checked her rearview mirror and saw the town ambulance with lights flashing, coming fast, so she pulled over to let it pass. When it made the turn onto Bumps River Road her heart took a dive. She feared little Angie Cunningham had taken a turn for the worse. She decided to follow and see if she could do anything to help, perhaps give Zach or Lexie a ride, or stay with the younger children.

Her car bounced down the badly paved road, which

led to the town dump and was lined with a mix of modest homes and the sort of unsightly businesses that town planners preferred to hide away, out of sight of tourists. There was a rather untidy masonry yard, filled with pallets of bricks and piles of rocks, a transmission service and auto body shop where a number of damaged cars awaited repairs, and a fenced in area boasting a shiny new cell phone tower.

Like the other houses on the road, the Cunninghams' house was a modest affair, a one-story ranch with an old-fashioned picture window on one side of the center doorway and a couple of smaller windows on the other. It was decorated for Christmas, however, with homemade wreaths on all the windows and a plywood Santa with sleigh and reindeer on the roof. A lighted Christmas tree was in the picture window.

Lucy pulled into the yard and parked next to a stack of lobster pots, taking care not to block the ambulance. She was just getting out of the car when the door to the house opened and the EMTs came out, carrying a stretcher containing a small, blanketed figure. Lexie followed, clutching her unfastened coat around herself and climbing into the ambulance with her daughter. Her face was white with tension, her hair uncombed. She'd probably spent the day anxiously nursing her sick daughter, finally giving in and calling for help.

Lucy blinked back tears, watching this little drama. She was so lucky, she thought, that her children were all healthy and so was her grandson, little Patrick. Oh, they'd had the usual ear infections and colds—Bill broke a leg falling off a ladder, and they'd had a bit of a struggle getting Elizabeth's asthma under control—but for the most part they'd all been remarkably healthy.

On the rare occasions when they had been sick or injured, they'd made speedy recoveries. They'd never had to deal with a life-threatening disease such as Angie's kidney disease, and the very idea made Lucy's heart skip a beat. She could only imagine how awful it would be to face the possibility every day that you might lose your child.

The ambulance was leaving and Lucy saw Zach was standing in the doorway, with the two younger children on either side of him. She gave him a yell and hurried across the yard. "Is there anything I can do?" she asked, reaching the front steps. "Do you need anything?"

The ambulance had been silent as it climbed Bumps River Road, but the siren wailed as it made the turn onto the main road and they could hear it as it sped to town and the cottage hospital.

"Oh, hi, Lucy," he said slowly, blinking as if coming out of a coma. Lucy realized he hadn't noticed her until now. "Thanks for stopping."

She repeated her offer of help. "Do you need anything?"

He hadn't shaved this morning, and his plaid flannel shirt and jeans looked as if they could use a wash. "No," he said. "We did a big shopping yesterday."

She could hear loud music punctuated with booms and whizzes coming from the TV inside. "Do you want me to stay with the little ones so you can go to the hospital?"

He shook his head, slowly and carefully, as if he was holding the weight of the world on his shoulders and was afraid of dislodging it. "No, thanks. I'm better here."

"It's no trouble for me to stay," Lucy said.

"Go on." He gave the kids a little shove. "Your show's on TV." They scampered off and he lowered his head. "Truth is, Lucy, I can't take the hospital. Lexie'll call, keep me posted."

"I understand," Lucy said. "Let me know if you change your mind."

"Thanks, I will," he said, closing the door.

Lucy made her way through the yard, past the faded plastic toys and the stacks of lobster pots, past an over-turned skiff, and got in her car. As she put the key in the ignition and started the engine it occurred to her that of all the people who lived in Tinker's Cove, the Cunning-hams had probably suffered most at the hands of Jake Marlowe and Ben Scribner.

Not only had Lexie lost much-needed income when her hours were cut at town hall, but the Cunninghams also lost their employer-subsidized health insurance be-cause she no longer worked the required number of hours. There were state programs for low-income peo-ple, but Lucy knew that these plans had strict eligibility requirements and she also knew that Zach's income from lobstering put them a hair above the income limit. Lucy's own family's health insurance premiums were al-most two thousand dollars a month, and they didn't have any preexisting conditions like the Cunninghams. Lucy wasn't quite sure when the new federal law con-cerning preexisting conditions went into effect, and that, she thought, was part of the problem. The whole health care system was a mess, a confusing jumble of co-pays and coinsurance and eligibility requirements that kept changing, and now the Cunninghams were at its mercy. Perhaps that was the worst part, she thought, the sense of confusion and uncertainty the system generated.

You never knew what amount you were responsible for until you got the form that explained the benefits from the insurance company, and in her experience it was always more than she expected.

If only Lexie had been able to keep her full-time position . . . The family would have the town's gold-plated plan, and they wouldn't have to worry about Angie's medical expenses. When you considered that Downeast was also threatening to foreclose on their little ranch house, the house they'd decorated so gaily for Christmas, it was more than enough to make a person very angry—possibly angry enough to pack a bomb into a holiday mailer and send it off to the person who'd taken away the family's medical plan.

Reaching the end of Bumps River Road, Lucy turned onto the town road and looked back at the Cunninghams' house one last time. Zach was a handy guy; she had no doubt he'd made the plywood Santa on the roof. He'd done a good job, too. Santa was freshly painted, every inch a jolly old soul, and the sleigh and reindeer were finely detailed. She had no doubt that Zach could put a bomb together, but she couldn't quite believe he would. She thought of his resigned expression as he watched the ambulance leave, and his admission that he couldn't cope with the hospital. If anything, she thought, he seemed a beaten man. Events had overtaken him and he could barely keep up with the demands of day-to-day life; he didn't have the time or energy for sinister plots.

When Lucy got to the rehearsal that evening, the church basement was a hive of activity. The cavernous basement room with a stage at one end, which was only occasionally used, had a dusty smell, a scent that Lucy always associated with amateur theatricals. Al Roberts was at the rear of the stage, banging away with a hammer, constructing scenery, and she was pleased to see that two of the three planned panels were already in place. Marjorie Littlejohn and Tamika Shaw were at the piano, working out music for the show. Sue and Pam had set up ironing boards in a rear corner and were pressing costumes and hanging them on rolling garment racks. Lucy greeted them, and asked if they'd found her costume yet, and Pam held up an extremely large blue dress with a lace collar and little black buttons.

"I think it will need to be taken in," Lucy said.

"Not too much," Sue said, casting a critical eye over Lucy's figure. "A dart or two will do it."

"She's terrible," Pam said with a laugh. "This was made for Holly Wigmore, and she's enormous."

"Maybe you can find something else," Lucy suggested. There seemed to be no shortage of costumes; she noticed a number of boxes and trunks piled up in the corner.

"We'll try," Pam said. "Or maybe you've got something that will do."

"All she ever wears is jeans," Sue scoffed.

"They're comfortable," Lucy said, noticing Rachel joining a little group of actors who were clustered on stage. "I better go. I think they're getting started."

"Break a leg," Sue said.

When Lucy joined the group, she discovered they were talking about Angie Cunningham. News traveled fast in Tinker's Cove, where everybody knew somebody on the rescue squad.

"Poor little mite," Marge Culpepper was saying. "What a shame she has to go through all this. She's spent more time in the hospital than at home."

"I can't imagine what her parents are going through," Bob said.

"And now she's been transferred to Portland. It's going to be very difficult for them," Rachel said. "They've got the twins at home, and there's the price of gas, not to mention meals."

"Portland? When did that happen?" Lucy asked.

"Around dinnertime," said Pete Winslow, a nurse at the cottage hospital who was playing Scrooge's nephew Fred. "She needs a kidney transplant and she needs it soon. We can't do it here in Tinker's Cove, so she's got to wait it out at the medical center. The problem is finding a good match."

"What about her parents?" Lucy asked.

"Of course they tried to donate, but neither one is a good match," Pete said.

"Maybe we could have one of those drives," Rachel suggested. "Ask people to volunteer to be screened. I'd be happy to help organize it."

"You've got quite a lot on your plate already with this show," Bob said, placing a hand on her shoulder.

"Donating a kidney seems like an awful lot to ask of a person," Florence said, with a toss of her head. "I mean, it's not like dropping a buck or two in the Salvation Army bucket. How many people would actually volunteer to go through an operation and give up one of their kidneys?"

"You might be surprised," Pete said. "A lot of people want to donate for a loved one, but they're not a good match, so they're setting up these exchanges where the organs are swapped out."

"What do you mean?" Marge asked.

"It's like this," Pete said. "Say your husband needs a

kidney, but you're not a good match. Somebody else, say in California, could use your kidney, so you donate your kidney and they fly it out to California. Meanwhile, somebody in Dubuque's brother needs a kidney, and that family member is a match for your husband. So your husband gets the Dubuque kidney, and maybe the California kidney goes to Iowa. I've heard of chains that involved more than twenty kidneys."

"That's amazing," Lucy said.

Florence put her hand on Bob's arm. "There must be quite a lot of complicated legal issues involved in something like that, aren't there?" She licked her lips and leaned toward him, as if hanging on his every word.

Bob cleared his throat. "I don't think so. The whole organ donation thing has become pretty standardized from a legal point of view."

"I've heard of people selling their organs," Florence said, widening her eyes. "Can you imagine?"

Rachel threw a glance in Lucy's direction, then clapped her hands. "Let's get started," she said in a sharp tone. "This is a rehearsal, not a gabfest."

Marge looked at her watch. "Oh, my goodness, is this the time?"

"Seven-thirty," Lucy said.

"The caroling starts at eight, you know," Marge reminded.

Rachel's jaw dropped. "Is it tonight?" The annual carol sing at Country Cousins was a long-standing town tradition and she knew that nobody wanted to miss it.

Marge nodded. "Barney's on special patrol, making sure people can cross the street safely."

"I've been so busy I forgot all about it," Rachel confessed. "No point continuing here. We'll have to reschedule the rehearsal." This announcement was met with approval from the cast, and people started gathering up their coats and hats.

"You're just canceling the rehearsal?" Florence asked, clearly displeased.

"It's the carol sing," Al said. "Everybody goes." He tilted his head toward the door, where most of the cast members were making their departures.

"But there's so much to do for the show," Florence protested, placing her hand on Bob's arm. "Couldn't we at least go through our lines?"

"You've only got one line," Rachel snapped, losing patience. *"Uncle, Fred will be so pleased you've come."*

Bob stepped away, going over to the coatrack and busying himself getting Rachel's coat. Lucy thought he'd made a wise decision.

"Are you sure?" Florence asked. "I thought there was more. I thought Fred's wife was a leading part."

"No, just that one line," Rachel said. "Trust me. Everything will get done. We've got plenty of time."

Almost everyone had left by now. Lucy had joined Bob, who was holding Rachel's coat. Al was standing by the door, where the panel of light switches was located, waiting to turn them off.

Florence wasn't convinced. She was looking at the unpainted flats that Al had erected on the stage. "If you don't mind, I think I'll stay and work out a plan for painting the scenery."

"That's really not necessary," Rachel said.

"I'm not much of a singer," Florence said. "And besides, I won't have time tomorrow. I have to take Virginia to the airport."

"Suit yourself," Rachel said, slipping into her coat and buttoning it.

"Don't forget to turn out the lights," Al said.

The four of them left the hall together, walking the short distance to Country Cousins. There a crowd had already gathered in front of the quaint country store that still sold penny candy, calico by the yard, and cheddar cheese cut from a huge wheel. The porch boasted two benches, one marked *Democrats* and the other *Republicans*, and in fine weather they were filled by old folks who enjoyed debating the issues of the day. The store itself hadn't changed with the times, but the business model had. Country Cousins had grown far beyond the original store and had become a huge catalog and online retailer, with shiny new state-of-the-art headquarters located out on the town line, near the interstate.

Nobody was thinking of that, however, as they greeted Barney and hurried across the road to join friends and neighbors and family gathered around the bonfire that was burning in a steel drum. Lucy spotted Bill and Zoe and squeezed through the crowd to join them. "Where's Sara?" she asked.

"At the college," Bill said.

"SAC meeting," Zoe added.

Then Dick Kershaw blew the first notes of "Deck the Halls" on his cornet and the singing began. It was a fine, clear night, not too cold. Gazing around at the happy faces, Lucy raised her voice in the songs she'd sung every year since she was a child. Some earnest volunteers had printed up booklets with the words to the carols, but nobody needed them, except for the tricky later verses to the "Partridge in a Pear Tree" carol. Then they were all singing the last song, "Silent Night," and almost everyone was gazing skyward, at the bright stars that dotted the sky.

"Oh, darn!" Lucy exclaimed, as the last note ended.

"What is it?" Bill hissed, his voice a mixture of concern and annoyance. "You're spoiling the moment."

"Sorry," she whispered back. "It's just that I left my bag at the church."

"No problem. I parked the truck over there."

"What about you, Zoe?" Lucy asked.

"I'm meeting my friends for hot chocolate at the coffee shop," she said, already on the move. "I've got a ride home."

"Not too late," Lucy said.

"Promise," she called over her shoulder, running to greet her girlfriends. Lucy watched them exchanging hugs and air kisses with all the sophistication of Hollywood starlets.

Bill slipped his arm around Lucy's waist as they made their way back to the church, on the other side of the town green where white lights had been strung in the trees. "That was fun, wasn't it?"

"It's my favorite Christmas thing," Lucy said. Then she added, "Well, except for the presents."

They were laughing together when they reached the church parking lot, where there were only three vehicles: Lucy's SUV, Bill's truck, and Florence's little Civic. Bill got in his truck and started the engine, but promised not to leave until Lucy had retrieved her purse and started her car.

Lucy went inside, calling out Florence's name so she wouldn't be startled. There was no reply, but all the lights were on, except those on the stage and the kitchen, which were dark. Lucy thought Florence must have left, forgetting to turn off the lights, but then she noticed her coat was still on the rack. Lucy spotted her forgotten purse on the table where she'd left it and picked it up, then decided to see if Florence was in the bathroom. A quick check revealed that the ladies room was empty, so Lucy returned to the hall and called Florence's name again. This time she got a reply, a faint moan that came from the stage area.

Lucy immediately ran to the switches and flicked them all on; the kitchen and stage area were now brightly illuminated. The stage was different from before, she realized. The big scenery flats that Al had constructed were no longer standing in place. They'd fallen, and Florence was trapped beneath them.

Chapter Eleven

"I'm coming!" Lucy cried, rushing up the steps to the stage. But when she tried to lift the flats off Florence she found they were too heavy for her to raise by herself.

"Hang on! I have to get help!" she cried, getting a moan in response. Then she was dashing through the hall and out to the parking lot, calling Bill. "I need help!" she yelled. "Call nine-one-one."

"What's the matter?" Bill was out of the truck and running across the parking lot.

"The scenery fell on Florence. She's trapped and I think she's hurt."

Then they were back inside and Bill was hoisting the first of the three flats that had fallen, one on top of the other like huge dominoes. Florence's hand and arm became visible. Then he lifted the second flat and her head and shoulders were revealed. Lucy was calling 9-1-1 and the ambulance was on its way when he got the last piece of scenery off the trapped woman, who had been knocked to the floor, face down.

"Don't move," Lucy warned. "You might have hurt your back."

"Thank God you came," Florence said in a weak voice. "I was afraid I'd be here forever."

Lucy reached for her hand and held it. "It's all right. The rescue squad is on the way."

"I think I'm really okay," Florence said. "It was just that I couldn't get out from under."

"What happened?" Bill asked, examining the flats. Each one was made out of two sheets of plywood nailed to a frame of two-by-fours. "Did you try to move them or something?"

"No," she said, her voice small.

Lucy gave her hand a squeeze. "There'll be time to figure out what happened later." They could hear the ambulance siren coming closer, and then the flashing red and white lights could be seen in the windows. The door opened and the EMTs took charge, slipping a back board beneath Florence and transferring her to a gurney. Then they were off, leaving Bill and Lucy in the empty hall.

"How could that happen?" Lucy asked.

"Beats me," Bill said.

"Maybe they were only set up temporarily, not properly secured," she suggested.

"Seems like a foolish thing to do, what with the rehearsals and people coming and going," Bill said.

"What if I hadn't forgotten my bag? What if we hadn't come back?" she asked, as they reached the doorway.

"It would've been a long, cold night for Florence," Bill said, switching off the lights.

On Saturday morning Lucy phoned Florence to see how she was doing, but her call went unanswered. She tried calling the cottage hospital, fearing that Florence had been admitted, but the operator said there was no Florence Gallagher listed as a patient. Somewhat reassured, she headed out to the grocery store, where it seemed she was spending a lot of time and money lately.

Her grocery bill was always high at Christmastime, she thought, with all of the extra baking supplies she needed. She yanked a cart out of the corral and headed for the produce department, pausing at the holiday display of nuts and candied fruits to grab a bag of pecans and a tub of mixed fruits, wincing at the cost. She picked up a bag of potatoes and, noticing they were "buy one get one free," added a second, then headed for the carrots. She knew that chuck roasts were on sale and was planning to make a pot roast for an old-fashioned Saturday-night dinner, and her recipe required carrots. The problem was whether she could get away with the cheaper conventional carrots, loaded with chemical fertilizer and pesticides, or buy the expensive, organic variety that Sara insisted on. Would Sara even notice? She probably would, Lucy thought, because she often snacked on carrots. Reluctantly, she picked up the two-pound bag of organic carrots, priced at a phenomenal six dollars.

By the time she was ready to check out she was crossing her fingers that she had enough cash in her wallet to pay for the cartload of food, which included fancy Greek yogurt, cage-free eggs, hormone-free milk, gluten-free bread, and organic chicken. Maybe, just maybe, she was thinking, it would be more economical to subsidize Sara's desire to move out.

She was adding a chocolate bar to her cart, telling herself that today of all days she really deserved the jumbo size, when she spotted Florence at the end of the aisle. She was leaning heavily on her cart and was moving slowly, obviously in pain.

"Nothing broken?" Lucy asked, hurrying to her side.

"I was lucky," Florence said, with a tight little smile. "It could have been so much worse. I got off with a few bumps and bruises."

"I wouldn't exactly call it lucky," Lucy said. "It would have been better if it didn't happen at all."

"I was lucky that you guys came and found me. I was afraid I'd be trapped there forever."

"I forgot my bag," Lucy said. "I'm glad we were able to help." She paused. "Do you remember what happened?"

"Not really," Florence admitted. "I was sitting at Bob Cratchit's desk on the stage, sketching out some ideas. Then I heard a slam, like a door or window blowing open, and felt a cool draft, and it seemed to come from backstage. I had that sense you get, you know, that you're not alone, and got up to investigate and . . . well . . . you saw what happened. I was crossing the stage to check the back door and they all just fell on me."

From what Florence was saying, it seemed that an intruder must have entered the hall, perhaps intending to damage the scenery. Or maybe that person had planned to attack Florence. But why would anyone do that? "You have no idea who came in?" Lucy asked.

"I don't even know if somebody was there or not. Maybe it was my imagination," Florence said.

"The church is really old and needs some work," Lucy said. "I bet a window just slipped down—it happens in old buildings."

"You're probably right," Florence said, grimacing with pain. "And stage accidents aren't uncommon. I went on Facebook this morning and quite a few of my actor friends said they'd had similar accidents." She lowered her voice dramatically. "The stage is a dangerous place."

"Life's dangerous," Lucy said, adding that chocolate bar to her cart.

"Chocolate! That reminds me—I need some baking cocoa for my chocolate cheese cake. I always make one for my open house." Her eyes widened. "I do hope you'll come. I have it every year on Christmas Eve and this year I'm inviting the whole cast. It's going to be a blast." She pursed her lips, as if savoring a secret. "Guess what? Uncle Ben actually said he might come, which is amazing since he always flat-out refuses. It would be so good for him. We have lots of food and plenty of wassail and it's just a terrific party if I do say so myself. Will you come?"

"I'll have to check with Bill, but thanks for the invitation," Lucy said. She wasn't sure she wanted to go. . . . Come to think of it, she wasn't really friends with Florence and she really didn't like the way Florence had been behaving toward Bob. And the notion that Ben Scribner might be attending was hardly an inducement. She turned her cart, heading for the checkout. "Take care, now. What do they say? RICE: Rest, ice, compression, and elevation?"

"Something like that." Florence put her hand on Lucy's arm. "You know, I hope you didn't think me uncaring last night, when everybody was talking about Angie Cunningham's need for a kidney."

Actually, Lucy had thought Florence had been rather

insensitive but wasn't about to admit it. "Oh, no. It's a very personal sort of thing. Not everyone wants to be an organ donor, not even after they die."

"It's not for me," Florence admitted, "but I do wish the best for that poor little girl. I'm planning to make a donation to the Angel Fund."

"Sooner would be better than later," Lucy advised. "From what I've heard the Cunninghams are really up against it."

"I'll do it today," Florence promised, slowly rolling her cart toward the deli counter.

When she got home, Lucy put the groceries away and began browning the chuck roast. While it sizzled in the casserole, she found herself wondering about Florence's relationship with her uncle, and thought it odd that Florence was so pleased that the old Scrooge might come to her party. It just went to show, she thought, that you never could tell about people. She thought that Scribner and Downeast were a blight on the town, but Florence was hoping to rekindle family connections with him. Lucy gave voice to a little hmph, doubting that she would be successful.

The scent of browning meat filled the kitchen and Libby had heaved herself off her cushion and was standing next to Lucy, actually leaning her shoulder against Lucy's thigh. "There'll be some for you," Lucy told the dog, wishing that the human family members would show the same appreciation for her cooking. Dinnertime hadn't become a full-fledged war zone, not yet, but Sara was stockpiling arms and wasn't above firing off the occasional warning shot.

That night, predictably, Sara opened fire and sent a missile whizzing into the demilitarized zone. "I found a place to live that's actually affordable," she said, helping herself to mashed potatoes. "It's only two hundred dollars a month—that's probably less than you're spending to feed me, right, Mom?"

Lucy thought of her grocery bill and nodded. "Those carrots are organic," she said, "so you better eat some. They cost almost as much as the roast."

"What does two hundred dollars cover? Does it include food?" Bill asked, holding up the carving knife and fork.

"Yes! Two hundred dollars would be my share of the monthly expenses."

"That doesn't sound very realistic," Lucy said. "Is it an apartment or a house? Where is it?"

"I'm not sure. I'd be going in with a group. It must be a big place 'cause it's a big group."

"Like a hippie commune?" Zoe asked. "That would be cool."

"Who's in the group?" Bill asked.

"Oh, Seth and some others from SAC."

Lucy's eyes met Bill's across the table. Beneath the table, Libby was noisily licking her chops, anticipating her dinner.

"Will you have a room of your own?" Bill demanded.

"What about your studies?" Lucy asked. "I'm afraid you'll spend all your time in meetings, planning demonstrations and making posters."

"Are there going to be a lot of guys?" Zoe asked.

Bill set the carving utensils on the side of the platter. "I think I need to see the place. . . ."

"And we need to know exactly who's living there," Lucy added.

Sara's eyes were filling with tears. "I knew you'd be

like this," she said, pushing her chair back and standing up. "You just don't understand! Changing the system is more important than getting good grades! It's not like there's any jobs for grads anyway." She threw her napkin on the table and marched off angrily; they could hear her stamping up the stairs and then slamming her bedroom door.

"She didn't ask to be excused," Zoe said, in her good-girl voice.

Lucy looked at her youngest child, so like an angel with her cheeks like peaches and her big blue eyes. It was just a matter of time, she thought, before she lost her innocence and became a combatant, taking up arms against parental authority just like her sisters and brother before her.

Monday morning found Lucy hard at work at the *Pennysaver* office, pounding away at the keyboard to finish up her story about how Downeast Mortgage profited from Marlowe's Finance Committee vote. This was one story that really ticked her off and her fingers were flying as she recounted how some of the town employees whose hours were cut and who also happened to have mortgages with Downeast were now losing their properties to foreclosure. At the last minute she decided to call Will Carlisle, the mortgage officer at Seamen's Bank, and discovered that his bank's policy was to offer forbearance to struggling mortgage holders.

"The thing is, if they come in before they miss a payment, we'll let them pay interest only for a few months, and that's often all that they need. If the situation continues—say the mortgage holder is facing long-term unemployment—we'll work with them and renegotiate the loan so it's affordable. We're a local bank and we don't see foreclosures as beneficial to the community or to the bank," he said.

"That's terrific," Lucy said. "It's a shame more banks aren't like yours."

"We're small, and the board members are local businessmen. That means we can be a lot more flexible than some too-big-to-fail outfit."

"What did you think of the demonstration the other day—the kids protesting student loans?"

"That's a different kettle of fish," Carlisle said. "Our hands are tied by the feds, but we're trying to figure something out. It's a huge problem. . . . These kids didn't realize what they were getting into. Everybody told them college debt was okay. Personally, I won't let my child take out loans for college. Bella's going to have to live with what we've saved and start at the community college."

"I'm glad to hear you say that," Lucy said, delighted to find her own views reinforced. "We're sending Sara to Winchester. She's got a scholarship and she's living at home, at least for now."

"Smart," Will said.

Lucy thanked him for his time and finished the story, which she sent to Ted for editing. That job done, she busied herself with other stories and didn't think about Downeast again until Wednesday morning when Ted sent the foreclosure story back to her, heavily edited. All the references to Downeast Mortgage had been deleted.

"I can't believe this," she declared. "I worked hard on this, and it's all true. I've got the facts."

"It could be coincidence," Ted said. "Marlowe can't explain himself. We don't know that he had any intention of foreclosing on those town employees."

"Well, what if I call Ben Scribner and ask him? I'll get a comment from him."

"He's hardly going to admit anything of the sort," Ted said.

"That's okay. We'll have him lying on record. It'll be obvious to everyone, because of what's happened. He can say that Downeast never intended to benefit from the FinCom vote, that it was only an effort to control town expenses, but nobody will believe him."

"I don't want you calling him, Lucy." Ted wasn't making a suggestion, he was giving an order.

"Why not?"

"Because it would be harassment. He's just lost his partner, under the most horrible circumstances. . . ."

Lucy thought of all the times Ted had made her call grieving survivors of auto accidents and house fires, insisting that she was only giving them an opportunity to honor their deceased family members. "But, Ted, you always say it helps people through the grieving process if they can talk. . . ."

"No. We're running the story without mentioning Marlowe's vote or Downeast Mortgage. This is a story about how the recession is affecting our town."

"But Seamen's Bank—"

"I know," Ted said. "And I wish to heaven I'd gone to them instead of Downeast when I needed money."

"Oh," Lucy said, suddenly understanding the situation. "I get it."

He shoved his chair back and grabbed his coat, leaving without a word of explanation. Lucy and Phyllis both watched him go.

"It's deadline day," Lucy said.

"He's never done that," Phyllis said. "He's never walked out on deadline."

"Do you think he's coming back?" Lucy asked, her throat tightening.

"I don't think so."

"What are we going to do?"

"You can put it together, Lucy," Phyllis said, sounding like a cheerleader. "You've seen him do it enough times."

"I appreciate your faith in me," Lucy said, "but I don't know where to begin."

"With the first page," Phyllis suggested.

"Okay." Lucy took a deep breath. "What we need is a big photo on the front cover, maybe kids on Santa's knee, something that says Christmas is coming. . . ." she said, thinking aloud as she opened the photo file.

Even as she worked to lay out the paper, clicking and dragging and occasionally swearing in a struggle to arrange ads and stories in what she hoped was an acceptable format, Lucy kept hoping Ted would return. The little bell on the door remained silent, however, and it was nearly two hours past the noon deadline when she finally shipped the file to the printer.

"Good work, Lucy," said Phyllis, who had been watching over her shoulder. "That page-one photo of the little Mini Cooper with a Christmas tree on top is real cute."

"I hope it's okay with Ted," Lucy fretted.

"He's the one who walked out, leaving you holding the bag," Phyllis said with a sniff.

"I'm not sure he's going to see it that way," Lucy said, arching her back and stretching. She felt completely wiped out, her neck and shoulders tight with tension, and she had a low-grade headache. "I'm done here."

Leaving the office, she headed for home where she recruited the dog for a walk. Libby was thrilled at the prospect of running through the woods, and Lucy needed to soothe her frazzled emotions. The sky was milk white, and it seemed as if snow might be coming, but Lucy inhaled the cold crisp air and marched along, swinging her arms and humming Christmas carols. What was it with that "Little Drummer Boy"? Once you heard it, you were stuck with it. *Rum-pa-pum-pum!*

When she returned home she felt much better. She stretched out on the family room sofa with a magazine and next thing she knew Zoe was asking what she should make for dinner.

Rousing herself, Lucy threw together a meat loaf while Zoe made a salad and set the table. Tonight was the FinCom meeting and Lucy figured she'd fortify Bill with his favorite dinner. After they'd eaten, Lucy and Bill left Zoe in charge of clearing up. Lucy figured she might as well take advantage of Zoe's willingness to cooperate while it lasted.

The meeting took place in the town hall's basement conference room, which was set up rather like a courtroom. The four committee members sat at a long bench equipped with microphones and name plaques. Facing them were several dozen chairs set in neat rows for citizen observers; most of the chairs were empty. At the rear of the room a TV camera was set up, operated by members of the high school CATV Club. As promised, Ted had assigned a freelancer, Hildy Swanson, to cover the meeting since both he and Lucy had conflicts of interest. Hildy wrote the popular Chickadee Chatter bird column.

Lucy and Bill seated themselves in the middle of the room, receiving welcoming smiles from board members Frankie La Chance and Pam Stillings. The other two members, innkeeper Gene Hawthorne and insurance agent Jerry Taubert, ignored them, busy comparing favorite golf courses in Hilton Head. Hawthorne, who was chairman, called the meeting to order promptly at seven o'clock. The first order of business was the reading and approval of the minutes from the last meeting. Once that was done Hawthorne moved on to the first item on the agenda: filling the temporary vacancy left by Jake Marlowe's death. When he asked if there were any volunteers, Bill raised his hand and so did Ben Scribner, whom they hadn't noticed because he had entered late and seated himself behind them.

"Very good," Hawthorne said. "You both understand that this is a temporary position, and that a permanent board member will be chosen at the town election in May?"

Both Bill and Scribner said they understood that was the case. Hawthorne then asked them to each explain why they wanted the job and what they thought the proper role of the Finance Committee should be. He asked Scribner to begin.

"Well," he began, placing both hands on the back of the chair in front of him and getting stiffly to his feet. "I'm volunteering to fill in for my deceased partner, Jake Marlowe. We were partners for a long time and it seems the right thing to do. We agreed on most things and I think he'd want me to take his place."

This was met with nods of agreement from the board

members, which Lucy thought was a bad sign for Bill's prospects.

"As you well know, Jake believed that the least government was the best government, and by that he meant the least expensive government. Elected officials have a responsibility to the taxpayers to keep expenses as low as possible, especially in these tough economic times. People are struggling to pay their property taxes as it is, and raising them would create an impossible burden for those who are living on fixed incomes. If I'm appointed, I will be a strong advocate for responsible fiscal policy and I will carefully examine the proposed budget with an eye to cutting wasteful spending."

"Thank you," Hawthorne said. He turned to his fellow committee members. "Any questions?"

They shook their heads, indicating they didn't have any questions. No wonder, thought Lucy, as Scribner's opinions were well known. She wouldn't be surprised if he managed somehow to foreclose on town hall and sell it to the highest bidder.

Hawthorne was busy making a note; when he finished he asked Bill to address the same questions.

"Thanks for giving me this opportunity," he said, by way of beginning. "I've lived here in Tinker's Cove for almost thirty years. We moved here when I quit my job on Wall Street to become a restoration carpenter. I'm self-employed, but I studied business in college and have a strong background in finance."

Lucy thought she heard somebody make a "hmph" sound. It came from behind them and she suspected Scribner was indicating that he found Bill's qualifications unimpressive. Bill was not deterred, however, and continued speaking.

"I have a somewhat more progressive view than Mr. Scribner when it comes to town finances. It seems to me that the recent budget cuts are having a negative effect on the town's economy. Christmas spending generally boosts local businesses, but this year people are struggling to meet their day-to-day expenses and have little left over for the holiday. I made a few phone calls before coming here and learned that the food pantry has seen a twenty-five percent increase in applications and is barely able to meet the need. My daughter has been leading the toy drive at the high school and she says donations are down while requests are up. We've all seen the foreclosure notices, and the for-sale signs that are sprouting up all over town."

Once again, Lucy heard that "hmph," a bit louder this time.

"It seems to me that cutting town employees' income is the very worst thing we can do right now, when we need to give the economy a boost. I understand that the Finance Committee can't solve all these problems, but we don't have to make things worse by laying off town employees." He paused. "Thank you for your time."

When he took his seat Lucy reached for his hand and gave it a squeeze. "That was great," she said with a smile. "Well said."

"We'll see," Bill said, keeping his voice low. "I don't think I convinced Hawthorne and Taubert."

Hawthorne asked if there were any more applicants, and when no one else came forward, called for a vote. Frankie and Pam both voted for Bill, and Taubert voted for Scribner, which was expected. As chairman, Hawthorne had the last vote.

"I'm in a bit of a quandary," he said. "My inclination

is to vote for Mr. Scribner, because I agree with him that it's important to keep taxes low, but if I cast my vote for him we'll end up with a tie. That means the decision would go to the Board of Selectmen, and I don't want to cede control of the committee to another branch of town government."

Hawthorne paused here, and Lucy gave Bill's hand another squeeze.

"Furthermore, I've known Bill Stone for a very long time and I know he's a fair and open-minded person who will give serious thought to the matters before the committee.

Lucy was holding her breath; the suspense was killing her.

"So I'm casting my vote for Bill Stone, with certain reservations. Congratulations, Bill."

Bill got to his feet, turned and reached out to shake hands with Scribner, who reluctantly obliged, then left the room. Bill turned back to face the committee members.

"Thanks for your confidence in me. I'll do my very best not to disappoint you."

"That's great, Bill," Hawthorne said. "Genevieve, here, our secretary, has some papers for you to review before our next meeting so you can get up to speed. Keeping that in mind, do I have a motion to adjourn?"

"I so move," Taubert said.

"Second," Pam added.

Hawthorne banged his gavel. "Meeting adjourned."

Bill received congratulations from the handful of concerned citizens who attended the meeting, and hugs from Pam and Frankie. Taubert gave him the briefest of handshakes, and Hawthorne had a few papers for him to sign confirming his appointment. Then he reported to Genevieve, who handed him a banker's box full of documents.

"All this?" Bill asked.

"And those, too," Genevieve said, indicating two more boxes.

"Righto," he said, stacking two of the boxes one on top of the other so he could carry them. "I can't believe you got me into this," he muttered to Lucy.

She picked up the third box and followed him out into the night.

Chapter Twelve

Pam was already at their usual table in Jake's when Lucy arrived on a snowy Thursday morning. Lucy wanted to ask her about Ted's abrupt departure the day before, but Pam wasn't about to give her the opportunity.

"Congratulations!" she chirped, as Lucy sat down and shrugged out of her parka. "Is Bill excited about being on the Finance Committee?"

Maybe, Lucy thought, Pam didn't even know about Ted's hissy fit, when he'd stalked out of the office, leaving her with the job of putting the paper together. Maybe it wasn't the big deal she thought it was. Pam didn't seem the least bit troubled. "Not exactly," Lucy confessed. "He's feeling overwhelmed by those boxes of papers he's supposed to read."

"My advice is to start with the most recent and work backward," Pam said. "He doesn't need to get bogged down in the details. He'll get the picture soon enough."

"You don't know Bill like I do," Lucy said. "He's taking this very seriously. And, by the way," she said, intending to ask if something was bothering Ted, when Rachel joined them.

"What's Bill taking seriously?" Rachel asked. She had several tote bags slung over her arms and had the slightly flustered air of someone who had a long to-do list.

"He got the temporary appointment to the FinCom," Pam said, obviously pleased as punch.

"And he's pulling his hair out, now that he's discovered how much work is involved," Lucy added.

"He'll do a great job," Rachel said, dropping her bags in a pile around her chair. "I can't think of a better person."

"That's the problem," Lucy said. "He really wants to do a good job. He wants to do the right thing. I don't know how he'll handle the criticism. You know, when some member of the Taxpayers' Association accosts him in the post office or gas station and chews him out."

Pam nodded knowingly. "He'll learn soon enough. You have to develop a bit of a thick skin. I listen and nod and sometimes what they say actually makes sense." She paused. "Not often, but sometimes."

Lucy and Rachel laughed as Norine, the waitress, arrived with a fresh pot of coffee. "Where's the black coffee?" Norine asked, referring to Sue's regular order.

"That smells heavenly," Rachel said, wrapping her hands around the mug and inhaling the fragrant brew.

"She must be running late," Pam said, answering Norine's question.

"You look like you're running on empty." Lucy was talking to Rachel, who had rested her elbow on the table and was propping her chin on her hand.

"I've got the show and Miss Tilley and the Angel Fund, and Christmas is almost here and I don't know whether I'm coming or going," she admitted, with a big sigh.

"You've got a lot on your plate," Lucy said, knowing that Rachel spent several hours every day providing home care for the town's oldest resident. "I can help out with Miss Tilley."

"I might take you up on that, Lucy," Rachel said, sipping her coffee.

Pam watched as Norine filled her cup. "Do you think we should order? Sue just has coffee anyway."

"I think so," Rachel said. "I've got a meeting at nine."

"Regulars all 'round?" Norine asked.

They all nodded and she departed, writing in her order pad as she went.

"Who's the meeting with?" Lucy asked.

"Actually, I'm seeing a counselor," Rachel said.

Pam's jaw dropped. "You are?"

Lucy was also shocked. "What's the matter?"

Rachel's face was a portrait of misery, and Lucy noticed her long hair needed a wash, and her nails, usually filed into neat ovals, were ragged and broken. "It's Bob." She sighed. "That's not fair. It's not really Bob. It's me. Things just don't seem to be working."

"Marriage is like that," Pam said. "Every once in a while you hit a rough patch."

"She's right," Lucy said. "Bob adores you."

"Bob takes me for granted," Rachel said. "And I see the way he looks at Florence."

"I think you're imagining things," Lucy said. "I know she's flirtatious, but he doesn't seem the least bit interested. If anything, he tries to avoid Florence."

"When he heard about the accident, he sent flowers," Rachel said with a sniff.

"Who's Florence? What accident?" Pam asked, mystified.

"Florence Gallagher. She's in the show. She's playing Fred's wife," Lucy explained. "I saw her at the supermarket, by the way. She's doing pretty well after the accident. Just a few aches and pains, no broken bones."

"Like I care," Rachel grumbled. "I wish that scenery had squashed her flat."

"What are you talking about?" Pam demanded.

"Some scenery fell on her Friday night. She stayed at the church hall to work on it while we all went to the caroling," Lucy explained. "Bill and I found her trapped under the collapsed sets and called the rescue squad."

"That was lucky for her," Pam said, as Norine set a bowl of granola-topped yogurt in front of her. "Otherwise she might have been stuck there all night."

"Would have served her right," Rachel said.

"Rachel, I really think you're overreacting," Lucy said, taking her plate of hash and eggs. "She's just one of those friendly people. She hardly knows me and she invited me to her Christmas open house."

"I've just got a bad feeling," Rachel said, crumbling her Sunshine muffin. "You know how it is—you just feel that something's not right."

"Have you talked to Bob?" Pam asked.

"Yeah," Rachel said, her eyes filling with tears. "I asked him if he was attracted to Florence and he got mad. He denied it, got all huffy and angry, and that's when I knew."

Lucy stabbed her egg with her fork and watched the yolk ooze out. "He protested too much," she said.

"Yeah." Rachel was fumbling in one of her bags for a tissue and Pam handed her a napkin. She took it and wiped her eyes and blew her nose. "I'm sorry. I didn't mean to upset everybody."

"That's what friends are for," Pam said. "Whatever happens, you know we're here for you."

"That's right," Lucy added, squeezing Rachel's hand.

The three friends were sitting silently, glumly studying their plates, when Sue arrived. "Have you heard already?" she asked, taking the last chair.

"Heard what?" Lucy asked. Sue was as impeccably dressed and made-up as usual, the very picture of country chic in a plaid jacket, corduroy pants, and chunky boots, but even her Chanel foundation couldn't mask the dark circles under her eyes.

"Sidra called last night," she said, naming her daughter, who lived in New York City. "Geoff has kidney disease."

The news hit hard. They all knew Sidra's husband, Geoff Rumford, who was a local boy, as well as his brother, Fred, who was a professor at Winchester College.

"Is it serious?" Rachel asked.

"He's still undergoing tests," Sue said. "But it can't be good, can it? You need your kidneys."

"Yeah, but people have two and you only need one," Lucy said, ever the optimist. "Maybe they can just remove the bad one."

"Sidra's going crazy," Sue said, accepting a cup of black coffee from Norine. "She says she'll donate one of her kidneys."

"What about dialysis?" Pam asked.

"That's what I asked Sidra, but she says they're trying to avoid that. It's pretty miserable. It takes hours and hours and it's painful and has side effects."

"I didn't realize," Pam said.

"Me, either," Lucy said, thinking of little Angie in the hospital in Portland.

"Sidra's having tests, too, to see if she's a good match."

"And there's Geoff's brother," Lucy said, thinking of Fred.

"I know." Sue's expression was serious. "I'm sure it will work out. It's just so worrying right now."

"Of course it is," Rachel said. "We'll keep them in our prayers."

Lucy nodded with the rest, thinking that health really was the most important thing. Suddenly her worries about Sara didn't seem important. She was smart and strong and healthy, and Lucy crossed her fingers, making a wish that she would stay that way.

It was snowing lightly when Lucy left Jake's. She usually took care of a few errands on Thursday morning before going into the office, so she took a turn through the drive-through and cashed a check at the bank, stopped at the drugstore to take advantage of a sale to stock up on toothpaste, and picked up Bill's shirts at the cleaners. None of this took a great deal of mental power, so her mind was free to wander and she found her thoughts settling on Florence Gallagher.

Lucy thought she must be pretty new in town because she only met her for the first time when she'd interviewed her about the children's books she illustrated. Tinker's Cove wasn't very large; there were only a few thousand year-round residents, and you got to know everybody, at least by sight. As she made her way around town, driving carefully because of the snow, Lucy wondered why Florence had chosen to settle in Tinker's Cove. She was, after all, an attractive, single woman, albeit approaching her forties, and it was hard to understand what drew her to the small coastal Maine town. It wasn't as if there were a lot of single people her age. As for employment, well, the prospect was bleak, pretty much limited to low-paying retail jobs. Lucy admired the illustrations she'd seen, but wondered if that produced enough income for Florence to support herself. Perhaps she'd come in hopes of developing her art beyond illustrations; Maine's incomparable beauty did attract a lot of artists. Or perhaps she'd come, thought Lucy, because she wanted to be near her uncle, Ben Scribner. Maybe he was her only relative and she wanted to take care of him in his old age. Maybe he was her richest relative and she wanted to make sure she got mentioned in his will. Maybe, Lucy thought, speculating wildly, Florence wanted to make sure she got all of her uncle's money and got rid of his partner.

That was simply crazy, way out there, Lucy decided, catching sight of the Downeast Mortgage sign and impulsively braking. She was in the neighborhood, she decided, so she might as well pay Ben Scribner a visit and see if the police had made any progress in solving the bombing death of his partner.

She knew she'd have to get past Scribner's secretary, Elsie, and had her line of attack prepared when she entered the reception area, but found she didn't need it after all. Elsie was not at her desk. Instead, Scribner himself was standing there, behind the huge expanse of mahogany, looking through an appointment book.

"Can I help you?" he asked, looking up. It was chilly in the office and Scribner was wearing a thick gray cardigan beneath his Harris tweed jacket.

"I was just passing," Lucy began, "and wondered if there have been any new developments concerning Jake Marlowe's death."

"The police are fools," Scribner said. "They couldn't find a lost cat, not if it wandered in front of them."

Lucy thought he had a point. "They have their ways,

procedures and policies and all that. I guess there are good reasons behind it all, but it does seem to slow things down."

Scribner sat down and Lucy thought he looked tired.

"You could hire a private investigator," she said. "Have you thought of that?"

"I have," he admitted, with a sigh.

"Did you hire someone?" Lucy was definitely interested.

He sighed again, a long sigh. "I can't seem to decide." He raised his head and looked at her. "Can you recommend someone?"

"Actually, I can. I do know of a woman in New York. She investigated the Van Vorst mess last summer."

"Sounds expensive." Scribner made the word *expensive* sound rather indecent.

"I would imagine so," Lucy agreed. She thought Scribner looked at least ten years older than he did at the funeral. "It must be hard, losing someone you worked with for all those years."

"They blew him up," Scribner said, with a haunted expression. "It keeps me up at night, thinking about it."

"That's understandable." Lucy paused, debating what to say next, and deciding to go for the obvious. "Maybe you should talk to someone who could help you sort out your emotions."

Scribner snorted. "Now you sound like my niece. She's always fussing over me."

"Florence cares about you," Lucy said.

"She's a nuisance," Scribner declared, with a flash of his former self. "I'm a businessman; I've never really had a family. It's enough for me to understand business. Profit and loss, interest and capital, those are the things

I understand, and I don't see what's wrong with that. You can't do anything without money. You can't start a business. You can't buy a house. You can't build a school. People forget all that. Nowadays making money and being successful are viewed as bad things."

"I think it's the lack of money that's got people upset," Lucy said.

"Exactly." Scribner nodded. "It doesn't grow on trees— what do they think? You've got to be prudent, careful. That's what Marlowe was doing. He was trying to balance the town budget." He lifted his fist and banged it down on the desk. "Since when is that a crime?"

For a moment, Lucy was once again eight years old, sitting at her grandfather's big mahogany dining table, and he was banging his fist on the polished surface, making the silverware jump. "The deficit!" he declared, his voice rolling on like thunder, predicting doom. "The deficit will be the ruin of the country!" Only this time, it wasn't her grandfather railing against the government— it was Ben Scribner, defending his partner.

"Do you think he was killed by a disgruntled town employee?" Lucy asked. "Someone who might have thought he engineered the layoffs in order to foreclose on valuable property?"

Scribner's face flushed darkly and Lucy feared he was going to have a stroke or heart attack. "Marlowe would never . . ." he began.

Lucy hurried to placate him. "Of course not. But somebody might have thought that. Maybe Harry Crawford, for example, who's losing his family farm? Or Phil Watkins, who built that energy-efficient house? Did one of them threaten Marlowe, for instance? Or what about . . . ?"

Behind her, Lucy heard the door open and felt a blast of cool air. "Goodness, it's cold out, but the snow has stopped," Elsie declared, hurrying to her desk. "Now what are you up to, Mr. Scribner? Messing about with my papers?"

"Just checking my schedule," Scribner answered, sounding like a schoolboy caught peeking into his teacher's desk drawers.

"And you, Lucy Stone? What can we do for you?" Elsie's expression was challenging, daring Lucy to explain herself.

"I was just checking on the investigation," Lucy said, knowing how lame she sounded.

"Well then, I suggest you go and talk to the police," Elsie said.

Lucy felt the ground slipping away beneath her. "I'll do that . . . Uh, thank you," she said, making what felt like a lucky escape through the door.

Outside, she stopped to collect herself. That woman was scary, she thought, with a little shudder. How did she do it? Talk about assertiveness training—Elsie Morehouse could write the book.

Lucy was opening her car door when she heard a honk and looked up to see Molly had pulled up alongside in her little Civic. Patrick was behind her, in his car seat.

"Hi!" Lucy greeted them.

"We're going to see Santa," Molly said. She was wearing a red Santa Claus hat over her long blond hair. "Want to join us?"

Lucy considered the offer. She had intended to go to the office but there was nothing pressing, nothing she really had to do today. Besides, she was still feeling rather resentful toward Ted. "Sounds good," she said, jumping into the passenger seat beside Molly. As she buckled her seat belt she felt her spirits rise, like a school kid playing hooky.

"I was afraid we wouldn't be able to go because of the snow, but it turned out to be just a squall," Molly said, zipping along Main Street and heading for the highway.

"Ocean effect," Lucy said, calculating that only about a half inch had accumulated on lawns, even less on the road. "Never amounts to much."

"I see blue sky," Molly said. "I bet the sun will be out soon."

Lucy cast her eyes skyward. "My mother used to say you could count on it clearing when 'there's enough blue to make a pair of Dutchman's breeches.' "

"That's a funny one," Molly said.

In the backseat, Patrick was humming a little song to himself.

The trip to the mall passed quickly and they got to Santa's workshop just as it was opening. In the past Patrick had been shy about meeting Santa, but now that he was three and a half he was beginning to be much braver.

"Do you know what you're going to ask Santa to bring you?" Lucy asked.

"Cranky the Crane and Gordon," he replied promptly.

"The rock group?" Lucy inquired.

"No, Thomas the Tank Engine and his many friends," Molly explained. "It's on TV. There are books, videos. . . . It's hard to explain the appeal but somehow it takes over their little brains."

Mother and grandmother watched proudly as the elf

opened the gate and Patrick marched right up to Santa and climbed on his lap. "Ho, ho, ho," Santa said. "Have you been a good little boy?"

"Most of the time," Patrick replied with disarming honesty.

"Well, that's pretty good," Santa said. "What do you want for Christmas?"

"Cranky the Crane and Gordon," Patrick repeated.

"We'll see what we can do, young man," Santa said. "Now smile for the camera."

Patrick smiled, the elf snapped the picture, and Lucy found herself forking over ten dollars for a copy. It was worth it, she decided, studying the image of the tow-headed, apple-cheeked youngster sitting on the lap of the whiskered, apple-cheeked Santa.

Molly wanted to do a bit of shopping so Lucy offered to take Patrick off her hands for an hour; they would meet for lunch at the sandwich shop. Lucy enjoyed spending time with Patrick, especially now that he was a bit older and they could have a real conversation. They walked along, hand in hand, discussing the displays in the windows.

"Why is that lady flying?" Patrick asked, studying a mannequin suspended on fish line.

"It's to catch your eye," Lucy said. "If she was just standing there it wouldn't be very interesting. Because she's flying, we're looking at her, and we can see her clothes and maybe we'll want to go inside the store and buy them."

"Pink is for girls," Patrick said, commenting on the mannequin's sparkly skirt.

"Mommy might look nice in that," Lucy said.

"Mommy can't fly," Patrick said very seriously.

"No, she can't," Lucy agreed, chuckling to herself.

After doing a complete circuit of the mall, including a stop at the toy store where Lucy bought Patrick a little car, they settled themselves at a booth in the coffee shop to wait for Molly. Patrick was busy coloring his place mat when she joined them, carrying several large shopping bags.

"Looks like you were successful," Lucy said.

"I found some bargains," Molly said, sliding into the opposite seat. "How's your shopping going?"

"I'm almost all done. I did it all online the weekend after Thanksgiving," Lucy admitted. "I didn't feel like dragging around to the stores, and now I'm glad I shopped online because the rehearsals are taking up so much time." She nodded at the shopping bags resting beside her on the banquette. "I couldn't resist a few small things, though, and I still need something for Bill. Something special."

"How's the show going?" Molly asked, opening the plasticized menu and studying it.

"Okay, I guess," Lucy said. "I hope we get a good turnout. If we make any money it will go to the Cunningham family for Angie."

Molly's eyes were big and sad. "I heard she's not doing too well. Zach told Toby they're afraid she won't get a kidney in time." Her glance fell on Patrick's shining blond head, bent over his little yellow car, which he was pushing with chubby fingers. "I can't imagine what Lexie and Zach are going through."

"Me, either," Lucy said, signaling to the waitress.

The western sky was a gorgeous deep red when Lucy got home later that afternoon, and the windows of her old house were aglow in the reflected light. Winter sunsets were gorgeous, with intense color, but they didn't last long, so Lucy made a point of taking a minute before she got out of the car to admire the rosy light, which suffused everything with radiant color, a violin concerto on the car radio providing musical accompaniment to the show. Then, when the light faded to pink and then to gray, she gathered up her purse and shopping bags and went inside.

The answering machine was blinking so she listened while she took off her coat and hat. It was Rachel saying there would be no rehearsal tonight, and Lucy was thoughtful as she unwound her scarf, wondering if Rachel was having some sort of breakdown. She dialed her number but there was no answer, so she left a message, then got busy hiding Christmas presents and cooking dinner. She was scrubbing some potatoes when Sara called to say she was staying at the college to work on a paper and wouldn't be home for dinner, so Lucy put her potato back in the bag. Then, before she returned to the sink, the phone rang again and it was Zoe, saying she was at her friend Jess's house, wrapping presents for the toy drive, and Jess's mom had invited her to stay for dinner.

Her potato went back in the bag, too. Lucy looked at the two remaining Idahos and thought this was going to be her future as an empty nester: two potatoes and two pork chops. It seemed so meager, she thought, used to cooking big meals when there were six of them gathered at the table.

Lucy got the potatoes in the oven and then set two places at the kitchen table, thinking that with just Bill and herself it seemed silly to set the table in the dining room.

As she arranged the place mats and silver, she considered adding a couple of wineglasses. Evenings alone were a rarity and she thought they might as well take advantage of the situation and enjoy a romantic interlude. She recalled Rachel's confession that things weren't going well in her marriage and thought she didn't want to start taking Bill for granted, always putting him off because she was busy. She didn't know if that was the root of Rachel's problems but even Rachel admitted she was doing too much.

"We're dining à deux," she told Bill, when he came home. "Do you want to open a bottle of wine?"

She was terribly disappointed when he declined, saying he wanted to get to work on the FinCom papers. He barely spoke to her when they ate, clearly distracted, and then took his after-dinner coffee up to his office, leaving Lucy alone with her mug of decaf. She cleaned up dinner and settled in the family room to write Christmas cards, trying not to feel hurt that Bill had rejected her.

Chapter Thirteen

Next morning it seemed the old adage about a red sky at night being a sailor's delight was true. The sun was shining brightly in a clear blue sky and the air was as crisp as it could only be on a winter morning in coastal Maine, hypercharged with oxygen and smelling faintly briny. The cold made Lucy's nose tingle as she gassed up the car at the Quik-Stop.

Harry Crawford was doing the same on the other side of the pump, filling his rusty old pickup and complaining about the rising cost of gas. "They say it's gonna go up to five bucks a gallon," he said, glumly watching the numbers scroll by.

"When I pay my bills, I make the check out to *Thrifty Gas Thieves*," Lucy said. "It makes me feel better but they don't seem to mind. They cash it anyway."

"Thrifty Gas has no shame—if they did they'd change their name," Harry said with a grin. He was wearing the working man's uniform, flannel-lined pants topped with a plaid wool shirt, a thick sweater, thermal hoodie, and a barn jacket. He had well-worn work boots on his feet and a blue knit watch cap on his head. "I gotta say

I've got high hopes now that Bill is on the FinCom," he said in a serious voice, as he replaced the pump handle. "I need to get my hours back or it's gonna be a real mean winter, that's for sure."

Lucy finished screwing the cap back on her tank, giving it a couple of extra twists, just to be sure it was tight. "He's been working hard, going over all the papers. He's determined to be fair, and wants to look at both sides of the issue."

"Oh, right," Harry said with a knowing wink. "He's a good guy, a working man, not like that Marlowe, who never did an honest day's work in his life."

Lucy pulled her glove back on and shoved her hands in her coat pockets. "Any chance you can keep the farm?" she asked. "Have you been able to work something out with Scribner?"

Harry laughed, a harsh sound, like a bark. "Bastard won't budge an inch. He says he gave me the money when I asked for it, and now that it's my turn to pay, I've got to do it on time or face the consequences. He didn't force me to take out the mortgage. He's held up his side of the bargain and I've got to hold up mine, do what I said I'd do or else I lose the property."

"That's too bad," Lucy said, who remembered Scribner saying pretty much the same thing to Ike Stoughton at Marlowe's funeral.

"Yeah. My granddad held on to the place through the Depression, you know. It wasn't easy, but somehow he did it. I wish he was still around to tell me how, 'cause I sure can't figure out a way."

"Times are different," Lucy said. "If it's any comfort, you're not alone."

"It's not," Harry said. "Crawfords have owned that

farm for more than two hundred years and I'm the one who's losing it. It's like I'm not worthy of the name."

"Don't think like that," Lucy admonished, alarmed at his depressed tone of voice. "Like I said, everything's different now."

"I don't know about that. Seems like the same old, same old. 'Socialism for the rich and capitalism for the poor.' "

"That's always been true, for sure," Lucy said. "But I think there's something else going on. Things aren't working the way they're supposed to. Take college, for example. When you get out of college you're supposed to be able to get a job. . . ."

"I don't know about that," Harry said, his expression hardening. "I never had that opportunity."

Lucy wanted to tell him there was no shame in not going to college, that she knew how smart and talented and hardworking he was and that she respected him, but she didn't want to sound patronizing. "Take it easy," she said, reaching for the door handle.

"Don't have any choice," Harry said with a shrug, pulling a single dollar bill out of his pocket. "I'm gonna try my luck on the lottery."

"You can't win if you don't play," Lucy said, repeating the lottery's advertising slogan as she got into her car. "Good luck!"

"I'm gonna need it," Harry said, waving as she drove off.

Lucy was thoughtful as she cruised down Main Street to the *Pennysaver* office. The way she saw it, the lottery was part of the problem, not the solution. It took money from thousands of low-income people, like Harry, and redistributed big chunks of it to a lucky few. Then again, she decided, pulling into a parking space, there wasn't much you could buy with a dollar anymore. You might as well take a chance on winning.

Harry hadn't looked too optimistic about his chances; he'd looked like a desperate man who'd run out of options. She remembered his expression when he'd said he hadn't had the opportunity to go to college and suspected he'd been nursing a grudge for a long time. The question was, she thought as she switched off the engine, whether or not that simmering resentment had driven him to construct a package bomb and mail it to Jake Marlowe. She would never have thought in a million years that Harry Crawford would do such a thing, not until now.

Phyllis was already at her desk, sorting press releases, when Lucy entered the office. "What's happening?" she asked, hanging up her coat.

"More foreclosures," Phyllis said, handing her several sheets of fax paper, all headed with the Downeast Mortgage logo.

"This is not good," Lucy said, speed-reading the legalese and looking for names. She didn't recognize most of them, so she figured they were for second homes owned by summer people. Too bad for them, of course, and not very good for the local economy, but she was relieved that none of her friends or neighbors were losing their homes. None, until she saw Al Roberts's name on the last notice.

"Oh, dear," she said, staring at the paper and checking the address.

"Who is it?" Phyllis asked. "I didn't have a chance to read them."

"Al Roberts."

"Like that family doesn't have enough to worry about, with little Angie waiting for a kidney transplant."

"Are Angie and Al Roberts related?" asked Lucy.

Phyllis's penciled eyebrows rose above her reading glasses. "Of course they are, he's her grandfather."

Lucy remembered how sullen Al had been at the last rehearsal, just before the scenery he had erected had fallen on Florence Gallagher. She wondered if he'd been so distracted with his problems—a desperately ill grand-daughter, a daughter struggling to keep her family to-gether with diminished resources, and his own financial troubles—that he'd been careless with the scenery. Or maybe, she wondered, he'd arranged for it to fall on purpose, deliberately striking back at Scribner through his niece.

The jangling bell on the door roused her from her thoughts as Ted entered, bringing a gust of cold air with him. "Glorious day," he said, unwrapping his striped muffler.

Lucy wanted to say something like "Glad you could make it" but bit her tongue. He was the boss, after all, and if he wanted to walk out on deadline day, well, that was his prerogative. Instead she said, "A nice day if you don't count the foreclosures."

Ted glanced at the sheaf of papers she was holding. "Who is it this time?" he asked, unzipping his jacket.

"Al Roberts," she replied. "And a bunch of second homes."

"Let me see." He took the foreclosure notices from her and began perusing, shaking his head as he flipped through them. "A lot of these folks are subscribers," he said. "We send the paper to them all year so they can follow local news. They're good customers, too, according to our advertisers. They order stuff from retailers year round and have it sent, they hire contractors to make repairs, they use heating oil and gas, they pay property managers to keep an eye on their homes." He gave the papers back to her. "It's not good for the town to have all these vacant houses sitting there."

"As if property values aren't low enough," Phyllis said.

"They're going to get lower," Ted predicted gloomily. "We haven't seen the worst of this."

"Isn't there something we can do to pressure Downeast?" Lucy asked. "Get our state rep and other elected officials to put some pressure on Scribner?"

"That's a great idea, Lucy," Phyllis said. "What about the banking commissioner? And the attorney general?"

"We'll start a campaign to save our community," Lucy said.

"Whoa," said Ted, holding up a cautionary hand. "Not a good idea. For one thing, I'm pretty sure everything Marlowe and Scribner did is perfectly legal. And secondly, I can't afford to get Scribner mad at me." He shifted his feet awkwardly. "I can't risk it. He can call my note at any time and there's no way I can meet that payment."

Lucy stared at him. So that was what was behind his strange behavior. "Didn't you read the note before you signed it?"

"Of course I did, and it seemed perfectly okay at the time because it got me a lower interest rate—a full point less than Seamen's Bank was asking." He swiveled his desk chair around so that it faced away from the wall and sat down heavily, making the chair creak. "Those were the days when you walked in a bank and the first thing they did was ask if you wanted any money and they asked how much and said, 'Just sign here.' I never thought I'd have any problem refinancing if he called the note. The value of the house was going up all the time, lenders were tripping over each other to give me money." He snorted. "I thought I was being smart. I never thought the bubble would burst."

"None of us did," Phyllis said.

"We can't just give up," Lucy said. "We have a role to play here. We need to get the facts out and mobilize people to save the town."

"If it's any consolation, there will come a point when even Scribner realizes the folly of foreclosing every time a borrower misses a payment. He's going to end up with a lot of decaying, worthless property," Ted said.

"By then it will be too late," Phyllis said. "Tinker's Cove will be a ghost town."

For a moment Lucy imagined tumbleweeds blowing down Main Street, an image straight out of a Western movie. "Instead of a showdown," she said, "let's try an ambush."

"Somehow I feel as if I've wandered into the Last Chance Saloon," Ted said.

Lucy grinned. "We could do a story about the Social Action Committee at the college, let them take on Downeast."

"That's actually a good idea, pardner," Ted said, brightening. "You could interview their leader—what's his name?"

"Seth, Seth Lesinski," Lucy said, reaching for her phone.

*   *   *

Seth was only too happy to be interviewed and suggested meeting at the coffee shop in the student union later that afternoon. Lucy was seated in a comfy armchair in the attractive space with orange walls and distressed wood floor, planning the questions she wanted to ask, when Seth arrived. He definitely exuded charisma, she decided, as heads turned in his direction. He paused here and there, grinning and exchanging pleasantries, as he made his way toward her, working the room like a pro.

"Thanks for coming," Lucy said, as he seated himself next to her. "Can I get you a coffee or something?"

"No, thanks," he said, shrugging out of his camo Windbreaker but leaving on his black beret and checked Arab-style scarf. She figured it wasn't just for the image of a revolutionary leader he was working so hard to project; his shaved head probably got cold.

"Like I said on the phone, I'm writing this profile for the *Pennysaver* newspaper," Lucy began. "I guess I'd like to begin by asking why you started the Social Action Committee...."

"I didn't start it," Seth said, "and I'm not the president or leader or anything like that. We have no leaders in this movement. Everything is decided by a vote of the members."

Lucy looked at him, wondering if he really believed what he was saying. He was no kid, she realized, noticing the lines around his eyes and a slight graying of the obligatory stubble on his cheeks and chin. No wonder he shaved his head, she thought, suspecting his hair was either graying or balding. "Okay," she said, "but you do seem to be the guy holding the megaphone."

"I know," he admitted, with a rueful shake of his head, "but I'm trying to change that. Nobody besides me seems willing to come forward, but we're holding some public speaking workshops and I'm hoping to pass the megaphone to others."

Lucy nodded as she wrote this down in her notebook. "Has the group agreed on any goals?" she asked.

"We want foreclosures to stop. We want action on student loans—they've overtaken credit card debt as a national problem. And we want the military budget cut and the troops out of Afghanistan." He paused. "That's especially important to me. I'm here on the GI Bill, you know. I was in the army, saw action in Iraq and Afghanistan." He leaned forward, making intense eye contact. "I saw my friends die and I was lucky to get out alive, and this is not the America we were fighting for. We didn't die and risk our lives so greedy bastards like Marlowe and Scribner could get rich by making people homeless."

Lucy was writing it all down, scribbling as fast as she could and wondering why she'd neglected to bring along her tape recorder. She knew why—she hated the way the machine intruded on an interview, making people nervous and stilted. "How many students are in the group?" she finally asked.

"We can draw quite a crowd for a demonstration," he said, looking satisfied with himself.

"But how many go to meetings? How many are actually committed activists?"

"Like your daughter?" he asked, catching her by surprise.

Lucy wasn't about to show he'd rattled her. "Like Sara," she said.

"You know, Sara suggested I contact you and ask to be interviewed," he said. "You called me before I got a chance."

This was very unexpected news, considering how irritable Sara had been lately. "Really?" she asked, her voice bright with pleasure.

"Yeah." He nodded. "She said it would be a good way to present our ideas to the public. SAC isn't just a college group, you know. We'd like people from the community to join us. We're fighting for them, after all."

"Traditionally there's been a sharp division between town and gown—do you think you can overcome that?"

"I hope so," Seth said. "All we're after is fairness, a level playing field. It's not right for one percent to own forty-two percent of the wealth in this country. It's not right that half the population is living at or below the poverty line. This is the richest country in the world and kids are going hungry, families are losing their homes. It's time that people stood up for themselves and demanded fairness."

"How far should they go?" Lucy asked. "Do you condone violence, like the bombing that killed Marlowe?"

"I would never condone violence; I don't think anybody who's been to war would," he said in a soft voice. His expression was troubled, his eyes were directed at hers but he wasn't seeing her, he was seeing something else, reliving a wartime horror. Then, with a shake of his head, he came back to the present. "If things continue the way they are, I wouldn't be at all surprised to see more violence. That's what happens when people run out of options. They get desperate."

"Let's hope it doesn't come to that," Lucy said.

He smiled, revealing large eyeteeth that gave him a wolfish look. "When hope runs out, that's when there's trouble."

Lucy had a few more questions and the interview continued for a little longer before she was able to wrap it up. When she had no more questions she asked him if she could snap a photo; he was happy to oblige. When she checked the image in her digital camera she thought it reminded her of something, and when she was walking across campus to the parking lot it came to her. He looked like that famous poster of Che Guevara, she decided, not knowing whether to laugh . . . or cry.

Chapter Fourteen

Friday night was pizza night, when the family gathered around the kitchen table instead of eating in the dining room. It was the one night when Lucy used paper plates and paper napkins, and the kids were allowed to drink soda. That had been more of a thrill when they were little, but there was still something special about Friday. Maybe it was just the fact that the work and school week was over, and they could look forward to sleeping in on Saturday.

Bill always picked up the pizza on his way home, and when Lucy saw his headlights in the driveway she called the girls. They came clumping down the back stairs and sat down at the table, waiting for him to set the big box in front of them. Wine was poured, flip tabs on soda cans were popped, and everybody dived in.

"I interviewed Seth Lesinski today," Lucy said, her mouth full of spicy cheesy tomato goodness. "He's a very interesting guy."

"Mmmph," Sara replied.

"He mentioned you. He said you're a 'committed activist.'"

"Sara?" Zoe scoffed. "He should see her getting dressed in the morning, deciding what to wear and fussing with her hair and makeup."

"I sure hope he doesn't see her like that," Bill said, and Lucy wasn't sure if he was joking or not.

"Da-a-ad," Sara protested, blushing. "It's not like that. It's a movement. Seth's interested in making history, not . . . you know, romantic stuff."

"Believe me, Sara, every guy is interested in, uh, romantic stuff." Bill reached for the bottle and refilled his wineglass.

"Why do you always think the worst of people?" Sara demanded, rising from her chair. "Seth is . . . Seth is amazing! He's not immature like the boys on campus. He's got goals and ideas. He fought in Afghanistan. . . . He's a hero!" Then she flung down her crumpled paper napkin and ran upstairs, where she slammed her bedroom door.

"I think she really likes him," Zoe said, finishing off her piece of pizza and reaching for another.

"I think you're right," Lucy said, deciding this could definitely be a problem. "Bill, would you please pass the salad?"

After dinner, Bill buried himself in his attic office with the FinCom papers and Lucy got ready to go to rehearsal. Sara didn't answer when she knocked on her door, asking if she wanted a ride anywhere, but Zoe asked to be dropped at her friend Izzy's house.

Lucy was a few minutes late when she got to the church hall, but the rehearsal hadn't started yet. Bob was conferring with Al Roberts on the stage; the scenery hadn't been replaced but was lying on the stage floor in a neat stack. Rachel was seated alone, going over the script, and a chattering group had gathered around Florence, who was holding court at the back of the room.

Lucy took a seat beside Rachel, who cast her eyes in Florence's direction. "You'd think she was the star of the show," she muttered.

"She's just one of those people who's got a big personality," Lucy said. "Bob doesn't even seem to notice her."

"He knows he better not," Rachel growled, causing Lucy to laugh.

"I don't think it's very funny," Rachel said, standing up and clapping her hands. "Places everyone! We're taking it from the top!"

Lucy watched the opening scene, set in Scrooge's office, but when the actor playing Bob Cratchit began stumbling over his lines and had to be coached, she found it tedious and began looking for some distraction. Spotting Marge Culpepper sitting a few rows over, knitting a pair of mittens, she went to join her.

"I hope those are for the Hat and Mitten Fund tree," Lucy said, referring to a tree in the post office that was decorated with donated hats and mittens.

"You know it," Marge said. "I've made six pairs, and I'm aiming for ten."

"Good for you."

"I like to keep busy at these rehearsals," Marge said.

"Maybe I'll take up knitting, too." Lucy was marveling at Rachel's patience when Bob Cratchit got his lines mixed up for the fourth time. "How's Barney?" she asked.

"Still helping the state cops with the bomb investigation," Marge said. She lowered her voice to a whisper.

"They're looking at that college radical, that Seth Lesinski. They think he might have ties to terrorists."

"He's ex-army," Lucy said. "I think he's the last person. . . ."

"You never know," Marge whispered, transferring some stitches onto a stitch holder. "It's hard for vets. Eddie had his troubles," she said, referring to her son, who struggled with drugs as a returning vet. "Sometimes they go a little screwy, get mixed up and start to sympathize with the enemy."

"That seems very unlikely to me," Lucy said, hearing her voice called. "I gotta go—it's my big scene."

"Break a leg," Marge said.

"Not funny," Lucy said, taking her place on stage with Tiny Tim. It was a brief scene, over in a minute or two, and when she exited Lucy found Al Roberts watching in the wings.

"How was I?" she asked.

Her question startled Al, and she realized he'd been lost in his thoughts. "Sorry," he said. "I wasn't watching."

"You must have a lot on your mind," Lucy said sympathetically. "How's Angie doing?"

"Not very good." He looked older than she remembered, and terribly tired.

"I'm so sorry," Lucy said. "Is there anything I can do?"

He shrugged. "They're doing everything they can at the hospital, but Lexie says they haven't got a match for her kidney and every day that goes by . . ."

"I know," Lucy said, biting her lip.

"I want to see her before . . . you know. She might not have very long."

Lucy wondered why he didn't just go. There was nothing keeping him here in Tinker's Cove that couldn't wait. "Why don't you go to Portland?" she asked.

"My truck needs a starter . . . and then the gas. It's pretty old, only gets about eleven miles to the gallon, and what with gas up over four dollars. . . ."

"Take my car," Lucy offered. "I'll catch a ride home with someone. No problem. I'll give you my gas card. Go."

"I couldn't do that," Al said, shaking his head. A number of cast members had gathered around them, waiting for their cues.

"Of course you can," Lucy said. "Let me get the keys for you. Stay here. I'll be back in a minute."

"No, I don't—" Al protested, but Lucy was already down the steps and hurrying to the chair where she'd left her purse. When she got back, Al stubbornly refused to take her keys.

"Please. It's the least I can do." She noticed Florence, who was standing nearby. "Florence will give me a ride home, won't you, Florence?"

"Sure," Florence replied. "Have you got car trouble?"

"No. I'm trying to get Al to take my car so he can visit his granddaughter in the hospital in Portland."

"Doesn't he have his own car?" Florence asked. Others had heard the conversation and were beginning to pay attention.

"Got car trouble, Al?" Bob asked.

"I know a great mechanic," Florence offered.

Al was distinctly uncomfortable with all the attention. His face was turning red and he was fidgeting restlessly, looking for an out. "I've got it under control," he said.

"Listen, if you need gas money, we can pass the hat," Florence suggested. "All for one and one for all—isn't that how it goes?"

"Sure," Marge said. "Angie should see her grandpa."

The group had surrounded Al, whose eyes had taken on a glazed look Lucy had recently seen on an aged lion surrounded by hyenas in a nature film on TV. "The man needs air," Lucy said, trying to give him an exit. Nobody paid attention; they were all digging in their purses and pockets for spare cash.

"Here, I've got five," Florence said, offering Al a neatly folded bill.

"Keep it!" he snarled, and everybody fell still. "I don't want help, not from any of you and especially not from her," he declared, pointing at Florence. Then he turned and stormed out of the hall.

Speechless, they all watched him go.

"What was that all about?" Florence asked.

"Downeast is foreclosing on his house," Lucy said. "I saw the notice today."

"Oh." Florence looked puzzled. "But why does he blame me?"

"Because of your uncle," Lucy suggested.

"Well, that's not her fault," Bob declared, defending Florence. "That's a legal matter between Al and Downeast. It's nothing to do with Florence."

Something brushed Lucy's shoulder, and she realized Rachel was standing beside her, leaning close. "Damn," she whispered, in Lucy's ear.

"I'm sure it's nothing," Lucy said, not sure but hoping it was.

"Oh, I'm not worried about *that,*" Rachel said. "I'm worried about losing Al. The scenery's not finished."

Right, Lucy thought, who didn't believe her for a minute. "I'll ask Bill. He can finish it up if Al doesn't come back."

Rachel squeezed her hand. "Thanks," she said, then clapped her hands smartly. "Places everyone! Act two!"

On Saturday morning Lucy and Molly went to the estate sale at Marlowe's place. The house was gone, the burned wood hauled away and the cellar hole filled in with dirt, but the huge 1866 barn was untouched by the fire and was still standing. It was also full to bursting with stuff, according to the newspaper ad, which promised: *C. 1810 tiger maple Sheraton four-drawer chest, C. 1820 drop-front secretary, empire card table, Civil War-era drum, muffin stand, tilt-top table,* and plenty more. What the ad didn't mention, and what Lucy and Molly soon discovered as they wandered among the pieces of furniture set out on the lawn, was that almost everything was broken and covered with a thick layer of filth.

"I suppose Bill could fix this," said Lucy, standing back to study the muffin stand, which was missing a leg.

"How would you clean it?" Molly asked, her lips pursed in disgust.

"Oh, lemon oil works wonders," said Lucy, who was trying to think where she could put the muffin stand.

"They're asking twenty dollars," Molly said, pointing to the orange sticker. "And it's just the first day of the sale."

"You don't think they're willing to bargain?" Lucy asked.

"Not yet," replied Molly, who'd just heard a woman's offer of thirty dollars for an enamel-topped kitchen table with a broken drawer, which was firmly refused. The table was priced at fifty dollars, which Lucy thought was wildly optimistic.

"Let's keep looking," Lucy said. "The ad promised old tools and I'd like to find something for Bill. Maybe one of those two-man saws, something he could hang up on the wall in his office."

"Maybe you'll find something inside the barn," Molly suggested.

The sale organizers had tried to organize the contents of the barn, but it was a daunting task and most of the stuff was still stacked in piles. Chests of drawers were topped with wooden crates full of junk and topped with three-legged chairs or bushel baskets filled with even more stuff. There were piles of old newspapers and magazines, stacks of moldy books, a child's rusty tricycle, empty picture frames, and cracked mirrors.

Spotting an old photo album, long forgotten in the barn, Molly began turning the pages and studying the pictures. "Look at this," she said, pointing to a pair of women, obviously sisters, dressed in long skirts and hats with enormous brims topped with feathers.

"They must be relations of some sort," Lucy guessed. "Maybe even Marlowe's mother or grandmother."

Molly closed the album. "It makes me feel like a ghoul," she said.

"Don't be silly," said one of the sale workers, a middle-aged woman who had been helping a customer who wanted to take a closer look at a wicker chair. Once the cobwebby chair had been taken down from its lofty perch, she brushed off her hands. "Marlowe sure doesn't need this stuff anymore, and to tell the truth, I don't think he thought much of it when he was alive."

"It doesn't seem so," Lucy agreed, looking at the vast barn. "So much stuff. Why was he keeping it?"

"Couldn't let go of it, that's my guess," the woman said. She was wearing a paper nametag that said *HELLO* in big letters. Her name, Liz, was handwritten in the space beneath. "We see this a lot. You wouldn't believe the stuff people hang on to."

"Such a waste," Lucy mused. "He had all this stuff but I don't think he had any friends. And he had pots of money but he lived in squalor."

"Well, we'll make a bit of money out of this sale so he's doing us some good. His ex-wife—she's the one who hired us—says she's donating her share of the proceeds to charity," Liz said.

"That's Ginny Irving?" Lucy asked.

"Right. She's a real nice lady," Liz said. "Do you know her?"

"I met her at the funeral," Lucy said, wondering if Ginny might be interested in helping the Cunninghams. She was considering how to approach her when somebody carried off a dressing screen, the faded and stained cloth in tatters, and revealed an old carpenter's chest.

"Excuse me," Lucy said, unable to wait to zero in on her find. "It's been nice talking to you," she added, over her shoulder, as she made her way between the piles of furniture. As she went she told herself not to get her hopes up. The chest was probably in dreadful condition and if it wasn't they would undoubtedly want a fortune for it.

When she got closer, however, she discovered the chest was made of mahogany, probably by a ship carpenter. It had rope handles and, once she'd wrestled it free of the milk crate of jelly jars and the potato baskets that were sitting on top of it, she realized the interior shelf with compartments for tools was in pristine condition.

"Those shelves are usually missing," Molly said, "or broken."

"Bill would love this," Lucy said, feeling a sudden, overwhelming need to possess the chest.

"There's no price on it," Molly observed.

"What should I offer?" Lucy asked, somewhat breathless with excitement.

"If it was in a shop, it would be five hundred or more."

"It's not in a shop," Lucy said. "And it's filthy. It's going to take a lot of work to get all this gunk off it."

"What's it worth to you?" Molly asked.

"A lot," Lucy admitted. "But I don't want to pay a lot."

"Ask Liz what they want."

"But what if they want hundreds?"

"I haven't seen anything over a hundred," said Molly, who had been studying the orange stickers. "Offer seventy-five and see what she says."

Lucy's heart was in her throat as she approached Liz, pointing to the chest in what she hoped was a nonchalant sort of way, and asking if she would take seventy-five dollars. To sweeten the deal, Lucy had the cash in her hand, three twenties, a ten, and a five.

Liz was busy counting out cash and making change for a woman who was buying several chests of drawers. She glanced at the ship carpenter's chest, narrowed her eyes, and nodded.

Lucy handed her the cash, restraining herself from

crowing as she waited for Liz to write out a sales slip. Then she and Molly each took one of the rope handles and carried the chest to Lucy's SUV, where they stowed it in the way back. It was only when they were driving away that Lucy allowed herself to celebrate. "Can you believe it?" she crowed, banging her hand on the steering wheel and shaking her head. "What a find!"

"Bill will love it," Molly said.

"I know! He'll be so surprised!"

Toby and Patrick were building a snowman when Lucy and Molly arrived at the house on Prudence Path. Lucy and Molly pitched in, and when the snowman was complete asked Toby for help with the chest. He carried it down to the basement and promised to clean it up.

"You don't have to do that," Lucy said. "I can do it."

"I'd like to do it," Toby said. "Let me. It will be my gift to Dad, too."

"Okay," Lucy agreed, relieved to cross that item off her to-do list.

When she went home, she tackled a few more items, including calling Ginny Irving about the Cunninghams.

"Their daughter is terribly sick. She's only ten, and she's in the medical center in Portland. It's difficult for them, what with gas being so expensive and having to buy meals in the cafeteria," Lucy explained. "As it is they're in danger of losing their home. It's a terrible situation and there's no one they can turn to. The grandfather's truck needs repairs and his house is in foreclosure."

"That's terrible. I'm happy to give them the money from the estate sale. I'd like to see it go to somebody who really needs it."

"The Cunninghams really need it," Lucy said. "The

Seamen's Bank has set up an account called the Angel Fund."

"Got it," Ginny said. "When I get the check I'll forward it to the fund."

"Thanks, that's very generous."

"Well, let's face it: Jake's life was all about making money and hoarding it. He stopped caring about people. I don't want him to be remembered as a miser. He was once better than that and that's how I'd like him to be remembered, as he was when I first knew him."

"It's very sad," Lucy said.

"I guess I always hoped that he would change, that he'd mellow when he got older," Ginny continued. "People sometimes do, at least that's what I've heard."

"He never really got the chance," Lucy said.

"That's true."

"Have the police made any progress?" Lucy asked.

"They haven't told me, if they did," Ginny said.

"Did he receive threats before the bombing? Anything like that?"

"We weren't close, you know. I didn't have any contact with him after our divorce and during my second marriage. Then after my husband died I had to manage our money, our investments, so I thought of Jake. That was the basis of our relationship. I'd see him about twice a year and he'd report on how the stocks and things were doing. He didn't get personal, except the last time I saw him, he seemed to be growing a bit paranoid. He was nervous and edgy and said something like, 'They're not gonna get me.' I asked who, and he didn't answer, but he said he was keeping a shotgun by his bed."

Lucy was genuinely shocked. "Oh, my goodness," she said.

"Looking back, it seems he wasn't paranoid at all," Ginny said. "It's not paranoia when they're really out to get you."

Chapter Fifteen

When Lucy got to work Monday morning the first thing she did, after flipping the CLOSED sign on the door to OPEN and adjusting the ancient wood venetian blinds to let in some weak winter sunshine, was call the Tinker's Cove Police Department and ask to speak to the chief. Jim Kirwan was polite as always, but Lucy knew it would be a challenge to get any information out of him.

"How are you doing?" he asked.

"Fine," Lucy said.

"And the family?"

"Everybody's fine."

"Is your oldest—the one in Florida, that's Elizabeth, right? Is she coming home for Christmas?" he asked.

"Elizabeth has to work on Christmas, but she's coming home the day after."

"So I suppose you'll be having two Christmases," the chief said.

"I'm really looking forward to seeing her. It's been six months since her last visit," Lucy admitted. "But that's not the reason I called. . . ."

"I didn't suppose it was," the chief said, switching to his official voice.

"I had a little chat with Virginia Irving on Saturday, after the estate sale at Marlowe's place, and she said that Jake Marlowe was extremely paranoid in his last weeks and that he kept a shotgun by his bed. He seemed to think someone was out to get him."

"These old folks tend to be a bit paranoid," the chief said. "I have one old lady who calls me at least once a week, convinced someone has stolen her silver tea service. I send an officer over and it's always in the same place; she just put it away in a closet to keep it safe and forgot where she hid it."

"Well, this is a little different," Lucy said, wondering how stupid the chief thought she was. "Somebody really was out to get Jake Marlowe, and succeeded! It sounds to me as if he'd been receiving threats. He knew he was in danger and he was afraid. So what I'm wondering is whether he reported these threats to your department. Did he?"

"That sort of thing would be confidential," Kirwan said, sounding even more official. "Department policy."

Lucy figured this meant Marlowe had indeed filed a complaint with the department. "I can understand the need for confidentiality when people are alive, but now that he's dead, I don't see how it matters," Lucy said. "Everybody knows that somebody really had it out for Jake Marlowe."

"I'm sorry, Lucy, but policy is policy. I can't start making exceptions—that's a slippery slope."

"How long ago did the threats start?" Lucy asked. "Did he have any idea who was making them?"

"I haven't confirmed or denied any action that Jake

Marlowe may or may not have taken in regard to this department," Kirwan said.

"Can I quote you on that?" Lucy asked in a sarcastic tone. She really hated when public officials resorted to speaking in officialese.

"Yes, you may," the chief said. "You can also say that the investigation is continuing and we are cooperating with the state police and the fire marshal's office. And this department is committed to following every lead and will not give up until the person or persons who committed this despicable act are identified. The safety and security of every Tinker's Cove resident is this department's primary concern."

"Is this an exclusive?" Lucy scoffed. "Shall I stop the presses?"

"That would be your decision," the chief said. "Nice talking to you."

"Same here," Lucy said, but her tone of voice made it clear that she didn't really mean it. Not that she'd actually expected to get much out of the chief.

She typed up a few inches, quoting the chief word for word, and sat for a few minutes staring at the computer screen. Then, impulsively shoving her chair back, she hopped to her feet, grabbed her coat and shoved her hat onto her head and headed over to the Downeast Mortgage office, pulling on her gloves as she went.

Elsie Morehouse wasn't thrilled to see her. "Oh, it's *you*," she said, adding a sniff that made Lucy wonder if she'd forgotten to use deodorant that morning. "Mr. Scribner is not in."

"I actually wanted to talk to you," Lucy said, grasping at straws.

"I can't imagine why," Elsie said, "unless you wish to

apply for a loan." Her tone of voice made it quite clear that she doubted Lucy would qualify.

"Not today, thank you," Lucy said, finding that annoying Elsie was rather enjoyable. "No, I came because I heard a rumor that Mr. Marlowe had received death threats before the bombing. Do you know anything about that?"

"I'm not at liberty to say anything about that," Elsie said, stiffening her back.

"Why ever not?" Lucy asked.

"The police said I wasn't to say anything to anyone about Mr. Marlowe, and especially not to the media."

"I'm not *the media*," Lucy said. "I'm just the little local paper. The *Pennysaver* is more like a community newsletter, like a nice, chatty note you might get from your aunt, or what your neighbor might say over the fence."

Elsie's face hardened and her permanent curls actually seemed to tighten. "I'm not a fool, Lucy. I know that whatever goes in the *Pennysaver* can be picked up by the Portland and Boston papers, and could even go on TV. And that's why I'm not going to say anything, because I don't want to get in trouble with the police."

"Who's in trouble with the police?" Ben Scribner demanded, entering the office.

"No one's in trouble," Lucy said. "I'm just trying to track down a rumor about Jake Marlowe."

"Marlowe's dead," Scribner said.

"But . . . but . . ." Lucy sputtered, as he walked right past her and into his office, closing the door.

Elsie peered at her over her half glasses. "Now, if you'll excuse me, I have work to do." She managed to give the impression that in her view Lucy was little more than a lazy layabout.

Lucy nodded, staring at the closed door. "Right, well, thanks for your time."

When she got back to the *Pennysaver* office she found Phyllis had arrived and was sitting at her desk behind the reception counter. "Did you have a nice weekend?" she asked, as Lucy hung up her coat.

"Yeah, I got a terrific ship carpenter's chest at the Marlowe estate sale. I'm giving it to Bill for Christmas. What about you?"

"I was there, too. I must've missed you."

"Did you buy anything?"

"I didn't find anything. It was all filthy and terrible. What a way to live, huh? And him so rich. Makes you think."

"It sure does," Lucy said, settling in at her desk and moving on to the Seth Lesinski story. She began the way she usually did, reading through her notes and highlighting a few quotes, organizing her thoughts. She knew it was important to be impartial and not to let her own feelings about the campus organizer color the story; the fact that her daughter seemed to be enamored of him was hardly relevant to the average reader. But she found herself recoiling when she read his prediction about violence, when he said, "I wouldn't be at all surprised to see more violence. That's what happens when people run out of options. They get desperate. When hope runs out, that's when there's trouble."

She sat there, her yellow highlighter pen in her hand, staring at the words. He'd really said them. She remembered the wolfish gleam in his eye and the casual way he'd tossed off the prediction. As if violence was inevitable, even natural to him. And she supposed it would be, after several tours of duty in Iraq and Afghanistan.

Sara saw him as a committed social activist, as someone who wanted changes that would improve people's lives. He said he wanted economic justice for everyone, which was hard to argue against. Lucy herself believed in the Golden Rule: Do unto others as you would have others do unto you. She figured that applied to economics, too, and that in a wealthy, civilized country like the United States everyone ought to have their basic needs met. She didn't want to go hungry and she didn't want other people to, either. She wanted a roof over her head and education for her children—those were things that everyone should have.

She was well aware that some people in Tinker's Cove were struggling financially, and sometimes weren't able to obtain basic necessities for themselves and their families. That's why she and her friends worked hard to raise money for the Hat and Mitten Fund, which provided warm clothes and school supplies for local kids. She wrote sympathetic stories about regional charities in hopes that readers would support them, and she was among the first to write a check for a good cause. She carried her beliefs into the voting booth, too, and voted for candidates whose views were most like her own. She also encouraged her children to volunteer their time to help others who were less fortunate and, she admitted to herself, at heart she was proud of Sara's social activism.

But there was a danger when social activists became frustrated and began to justify violence, which was what Seth Lesinski had done. Protests and demonstrations were one thing, sending a postal bomb was another, and she wondered if Seth Lesinski had confused the two. Had he taken his social activism a step too far? Had he threatened Marlowe, or perhaps even sent the package bomb? It was a disquieting thought, and the fact that Sara was involved with him made it even more disturbing.

Lucy was sitting there, wondering how she could convince Sara that Seth might be a dangerous person, and that it might be wise to step back a bit. She remembered how her earlier attempts had failed and was trying to think of a way to reach her daughter when Ted blew in.

"Writer's block?" he asked, noticing that she wasn't typing.

"Not exactly," Lucy said. "I could write a book on this particular subject, but I don't want to get sued for libel!"

As the day wore on the weak morning sunshine faded and the sky filled with thick, threatening clouds. The streetlights on Main Street had turned on when Lucy left for home around four o'clock, and a light snow was falling, the dancing flakes catching and reflecting the lamplight. She was planning on making spaghetti and meatballs for supper and decided to pick up a bottle of chianti. It was just the sort of night that called for a bottle of red wine.

Bill agreed when he got home and promptly opened the bottle, so they could share a drink while Lucy cooked dinner. It had been a while since they'd really had a chance to talk and Lucy found herself voicing her concerns about Seth Lesinski.

"He's not a kid. He's done several tours in Iraq and Afghanistan," she said, stirring the spaghetti into a pot of boiling water. "I can't imagine what he might have seen and done over there."

Bill was thoughtful, sitting at the round golden oak

table and sipping his wine. "Sara sure thinks a lot of him," he said.

"Of course!" The words came out like a small explosion. "He's a man, he's a hero, a warrior, and he makes these eighteen-year-olds who've never been out of Maine look pretty pathetic in comparison. And he has ideals." Lucy sipped her wine. "Ideals are sexy."

"Do you think Sara is involved with him?"

"I don't know," Lucy admitted, "but I do know that she'd like to be!"

Bill stared glumly into his empty wineglass, and reached for the bottle to refill it.

The storm was picking up when they gathered at the candlelit table and they could hear the wind howling outside. "They're forecasting at least a foot," Zoe said, who was studying meteorology in school. "It's a classic nor'easter."

"I wonder if school will be closed tomorrow," Lucy mused. "Classes might even be canceled at Winchester."

"That would be great," Sara said. "I've got a biology quiz tomorrow."

"Better study anyway," Bill advised, "just to be on the safe side."

"It won't be a waste. You'll need to know the material for your final," Lucy said.

Sara rolled her eyes. "It's under control, Mom," she said, helping herself to salad.

Bill, who was well into his third glass of wine, glared at his daughter. "Don't talk to your mother like that," he said.

"I didn't mean anything," Sara muttered.

Zoe was silent, keeping a low profile.

"It's all right," Lucy said, filling Bill's plate with a big pile of pasta. "This is a new meatball recipe. I got it from Lydia Volpe," she added.

"It's really good," Zoe said, eager to keep the peace.

"How are your grades?" Bill demanded. "College isn't like high school. We don't even get to see your grades, even though we're paying a small fortune for you to go."

Sara was shoving a meatball around on her plate with her fork. "They're okay. I'm not failing or anything like that."

"But they're not great?" Bill asked, pressing the issue.

"It's a lot harder than high school," Sara said, her voice rising defensively.

"Maybe you should make an appointment with your advisor," Lucy suggested. "What subject are you having trouble in?"

"Mostly biology," Sara said. "And I don't know why I ever signed up for Chinese—it's impossible."

"Not for millions of Chinese; they manage to speak it," Bill said. "Maybe you need to work harder. You could try studying instead of demonstrating."

Lucy inhaled sharply. This wasn't turning out to be the pleasant, relaxing dinner she'd hoped for. "Let's talk about this later," she urged. "I'm sure we can figure out a way to salvage Sara's first semester."

"I don't know if college is worth it," Sara declared, voicing her frustration. "You can't get a job, even with a degree. I think I'd be better off working for the movement."

"You don't mean that," Lucy said, horrified.

"I do! I don't see the point of all this studying. What good is it? What does it matter if I know what *ontogeny recapitulates phylogeny* means? Who actually cares about some silly, outdated theory?"

"I care," Lucy said, though she hadn't the vaguest idea what Sara was talking about.

"And so do I, dammit," Bill said, banging his fist on the table. "And I'll tell you another thing. You'd be smart to get as far away from those college radicals as you can. That's the sort of thing that can haunt you in later life, especially now when everything is on the Web. Some HR person will Google your name and a photo of you and that Seth Lesinski will pop up and you'll be branded some sort of radical and you won't get the job."

"If that's true, it's too late because I've already been photographed with crazy radicals," Sara said, yanking her napkin off her lap and throwing it on the table.

"Well, you better stop seeing them," Bill yelled. "In fact, as your father, I forbid you to see them."

Sara was on her feet, eyes blazing. "You can't do that."

"Oh, yes I can," Bill insisted. "As long as you're living under my roof you're going to abide by my rules!"

"We'll see about that," Sara said, turning and marching out of the room.

The three of them sat in silence, listening as she climbed the stairs and went to her room. Lucy braced for the slam of the door, but it never came. All she heard was the click of the latch.

It was Zoe who finally spoke. "What's for dessert?" she asked.

Lucy didn't expect to sleep well when she went to bed that night, and she did have trouble falling asleep, but once she drifted off she slept soundly. At one point she thought she heard an engine or motor, and the sound of wheels going back and forth on snow, and decided it must be a town snowplow out on Red Top Road. It was only when morning came that she discovered her mistake.

"Mom!" It was Zoe, and Lucy knew something was very wrong. "Mom!"

She tossed back the covers and ran into the hall, where she found Zoe standing in the doorway to Sara's room.

"Look!" She was pointing at Sara's bed, still neatly made. "She's gone! Sara's gone!"

Lucy ran to the window, where she saw a single line of footsteps through the snow, and tire tracks in the driveway. That wasn't a snowplow she'd heard in the night; it was a car. Sara had called a friend to pick her up. Sara had run away!

Chapter Sixteen

"Bill! Bill! Wake up!" Lucy shook Bill's shoulder and he groaned, shrugging her off and rolling over, pulling a pillow over his head.

"Sara's run away!" Lucy was insistent. This was a family crisis. "You've got to do something!"

Bill swatted the pillow away and rolled onto his back. "Sara's gone?" he asked.

"Yes! She never slept in her bed last night."

This information did not get the reaction Lucy expected. "Well, she couldn't have gotten far in that storm. Is it still snowing?"

"No. There's about nine or ten inches on the ground. Somebody must have picked her up in the night. There's tire tracks in the driveway."

"Must've had four-wheel drive," Bill said.

"Well, that does narrow the field of suspects," Lucy said sarcastically. Most everybody in town had at least one four-wheel drive vehicle.

"She's obviously with a friend. She'll come home when she gets tired of couch surfing," Bill said, yawning. "You know, I could do with some pancakes this morning. Fuel for shoveling."

"Make 'em yourself," Lucy growled, disgusted.

"What? What's the matter?" Bill was truly puzzled.

"Your daughter could be out there in the cold, stuck in a snowdrift, freezing to death, and you want pancakes for breakfast! That's what's the matter!"

"Be realistic, Lucy. She's probably sipping a cappuccino in the college coffee shop, telling her friends all about her horrible parents who don't understand her." Bill was on his feet, yawning and scratching his stomach. "Any chance of those pancakes?"

Lucy glared at him, turned on her heels and marched out of the bedroom. She was down the stairs in a flash, throwing on her coat and hat and scarf and gloves and boots as fast as she could, right over her plaid flannel pajamas. Libby watched anxiously from her dog bed, fearful that all this unusual early morning activity might somehow mean her food dish would remain empty. Then Lucy grabbed the keys to Bill's truck from the hook by the door and marched outside, into the clear, cold morning.

The snow wasn't as deep as she thought, she discovered when she stepped off the porch, and it had drifted somewhat, leaving only a few inches in the driveway. That was no problem for the pickup, and she made it to the road without any trouble. The Tinker's Cove Highway Department had been plowing all night and the road was clear all the way to Winchester College.

Suspecting that Bill might actually be right, she parked in the visitor's lot and went straight to the coffee shop, which was crowded with students and faculty buying take-out cups to carry to their eight o'clock classes. She scanned the faces eagerly but Sara's was not among them. Lucy did spot Fred Rumford, who was a professor, adding cream and sugar to his stainless steel commuter mug of coffee. She greeted him and asked if he'd seen Sara.

"No. I don't think she has any early classes," he said, shoving his glasses back up his nose. "I've never seen her on campus this early, anyway."

"I just thought she might be here," Lucy said, looking around.

"Family crisis?" Fred asked.

"You could say that," Lucy said, suddenly remembering that Fred had a much bigger problem in his family. She'd just learned a few days earlier that his younger brother, Geoff, was ill and needed a kidney transplant. "Oh, forgive me!" she exclaimed. "How is Geoff?"

Fred shrugged and sipped his coffee. "Doing okay, for the time being. They're looking for a match, but no luck so far. I got tested but I'm no good. Apparently nobody in the family is suitable."

"That's too bad," Lucy said. "I suppose there's dialysis."

"They're trying to avoid that. They say he's a really good candidate for a transplant. They just have to find him a kidney. He's on a list, so it's just a matter of time."

"I'll be keeping him in my thoughts," Lucy said. "And if you see Sara, will you give me a call?"

"Do you want me to give her a message?" he asked, looking concerned. "Tell her to call home?"

"Uh, no," Lucy said, imagining how negatively Sara would react to such a request. "I just want to know she's okay."

Fred nodded. "That's probably the best course of action. Give her some room and she'll come to her senses."

"Thanks," Lucy said, wishing she shared Fred's optimism. She was considering her next step when she noticed the coffee shop's enticing smell and decided she might as well have a cup while she considered her options. She got herself a double Colombian and took a seat at the cushioned banquette that ran along the café walls. After a couple of sips of coffee her head seemed to clear and she decided to do the obvious thing, wondering why on earth she hadn't thought to simply call Sara on her cell phone. She rummaged in her big purse and found her phone, took a deep breath and scrolled down her list of contacts until she got to Sara, then hit Send.

She got voice mail, so she left a message. "Hi! It's Mom. Just want to know that you're okay. Give me a call, send me a text. Whatever works for you. Love ya, bye."

Flipping the phone closed, she realized she hadn't felt this low in a really long time. She might as well wallow in it, she decided, staring into her coffee. She'd give herself until she finished the coffee and then she'd pick herself up and get on with her life.

When she drank the last swallow, she'd worked through her emotions, beginning with self-pity (*I'm the world's worst mother.*), gradually transitioning to resentment (*I may not be the world's greatest mother but I don't deserve this.*), and concluding with a surge of anger *(The nerve of that girl!).* She decided to take a quick tour around the quad, just in case she might see Sara, and had reached the science building when she slid on a patch of ice. A kid grabbed her arm, saving her from a nasty spill, and she looked up to thank him, recognizing Abe Goode. He was one of Sara's friends, and he'd even come to the house for dinner a couple of times.

"Mrs. Stone! Are you okay?" he asked. Abe was a big guy, a freckle-faced carrot top, wearing one of those Peruvian knit caps with ear flaps, and he was carrying a pair of cross-country skis over his shoulder.

"I'm fine. Thanks for catching me."

"No problem. This snow's something, isn't it? Fresh powder. I can't wait to get out on the trails."

"What about your classes?" she asked.

"I'll get the notes from somebody," he said. "No problem."

"Say, you haven't seen Sara this morning, have you?" Lucy asked. "I need to talk to her."

"I haven't seen her, but she texted me that she's moved in with that gang on Shore Road."

"Shore Road?"

"Yeah, the social action crowd, Seth Lesinski and his buds. They've got a squat there in a foreclosed house. Some kind of protest." He scratched the stubble on his chin. "It's not my thing. Talk, talk, talk, when you could be skiing."

Lucy smiled. "You've got a point."

Back in the truck, Lucy weighed her options. She finally decided to go to the squat in her role as an investigative reporter. If Sara just happened to be there, it would be a coincidence. She wasn't going there in search of Sara; she was just following up on a tip for her story about Seth Lesinski. And if Sara believed that, she decided, she might just try to sell her the Brooklyn Bridge.

Shore Road, which meandered along a rocky bluff fronting the ocean, was the town's gold coast. It was lined with huge shingled "cottages" built as summer homes in the early 1900s, as well as more modern mansions notable for their numerous bathrooms and ballroom-sized kitchens. One recently constructed vacation home, she'd heard, had eight bedrooms and twelve bathrooms, which made her wonder if the owner had been over-toilet-trained as a child. All the houses, old and new, had amazing ocean views, and most were empty for ten months of the year.

Lucy had no difficulty finding the squat; it was the house with eleven cars in the driveway. She added Bill's truck to the collection and made her way up the snowy path trodden by numerous feet and onto the spacious porch. The door, surprisingly, was ajar on this cold winter day. She stepped inside the enormous hallway, with its curving stairway and gigantic chandelier, and yelled hello, her voice echoing through the cold, empty rooms that had been stripped of furniture and personal effects.

"Hey, welcome," a girl with long blond hair said. Dressed in jeans and several sweaters, she was carrying an armload of firewood.

"Is Seth here?" Lucy asked. "I'm from the local newspaper."

"Cool," the girl said. "Follow me." She led the way into a large living room where a fire was burning in the fireplace, and a collection of air mattresses and cheap plastic lawn furniture was filled with a motley crew of youthful activists. Seth was leading a discussion, pointing to a whiteboard filled with economic terms: national debt, CEO salaries, progressive taxation, redistribution of wealth, economic justice. He paused, greeting her. "Hi, Lucy. Everyone, this is Lucy Stone, from the newspaper."

"Hi, Lucy," they all chorused.

"I don't want to interrupt," Lucy said, scanning the group and looking for Sara. "I just have a follow-up question."

"Right. We'll go in the library." He led the way through the group, and Lucy followed, but she didn't see Sara. Once inside the adjacent room, where the walls were lined with empty bookshelves, he turned to face her. "What did you want to ask me?"

"Well, for one thing, what's going on here?" she asked.

"The house is abandoned, it's in foreclosure, and we want to make the point that people are being forced out of their homes, being made homeless, when there are plenty of empty houses. There's no need for anybody to be homeless. The answer is simple: put the homeless people in empty houses."

"I don't think it's that simple," Lucy said. "Somebody owns this house. It isn't yours."

"A bank owns it. What's the bank going to do with a house? The bank can't move into a house," Seth said.

"What you're doing is illegal," Lucy said. "You're trespassing. What are you going to do when the cops come to evict you all?"

"Nonviolent resistance," Seth said. "I hope you'll cover it, when they come."

"Absolutely." Lucy added as if it were merely an afterthought, "By the way, is my daughter Sara here?"

"I'm not sure," Seth said. "We've got quite a crowd. Some are in the kitchen, making soup for lunch. Maybe she's there." He cocked his head toward the other room, where the group was waiting for him. "I gotta go. We're having a planning meeting."

"Right," Lucy said. "Thanks for your time."

He went back to the meeting and Lucy wandered out into the hall, searching for the kitchen. She found it in the back of the house, flooded with sunlight and featuring ocean views, and she found Sara, too. She was standing at the expansive granite-topped center island, chopping carrots, next to a Coleman camp stove topped with a huge, steaming stockpot.

"Hi," Lucy said.

"What are you doing here?" Sara demanded, her voice bristling with resentment.

"Just checking that you're okay."

"Well, as you can see, I'm fine."

"Great," Lucy said. "I think you should consider coming home."

"Why do you think that? I'm happy here, with my friends. We're doing something important."

"This is illegal. Sooner or later the cops will come and arrest everyone."

"So what?"

"Trust me, you won't like it. Jail's no fun, not even for a few hours, or a night."

"Well, I'm ready to make sacrifices for my beliefs," she said self-righteously, tossing her head.

Lucy sighed. "All right. It's up to you." She went to the door. "Give me a call now and then, okay?"

Sara didn't answer.

Lucy didn't know what to think, or feel, when she got back in the truck and headed home. She was running late, now, and needed to get out of her pajamas before she went to work.

Kids, she thought, shifting into reverse and backing the truck out onto Shore Road. She loved Sara, of course she did, but at this moment she'd cheerfully throttle the ungrateful little witch. She'd been through similar crises before, she remembered, driving the familiar route. Toby had dropped out of college after a single year in which he'd concentrated on partying rather than studying and ended up on academic probation. And there had been numerous flare-ups, especially arguments with his father, that had made his teen years rather difficult.

Elizabeth hadn't exactly been easy, either. She'd insisted on chopping her hair into spikes and wore only black during her senior year of high school, and had developed a surly attitude toward other family members. Her grades had always been good, though, and she continued to succeed academically at Chamberlain College in Boston, although she did have a few unfortunate conflicts with the dean.

Lucy didn't know why she'd expected things to be any different with Sara, but she now knew she'd been lulled into complacency by her third child's easygoing nature. Easygoing until now, she thought, flipping on the signal and turning into her driveway.

The house was empty. Only Libby was home, greeting her with a wagging tail and a big, toothy dog smile. You could always count on your dog, she thought, scratching Libby behind her velvety ears.

There was a note stuck on the fridge with a magnet, from Zoe. It was just a big heart, with a Z in the middle. Lucy smiled when she spotted it, trying hard to ignore the evil little voice that was telling her, "She's a sweetie now, but just wait a few years!"

Minutes later, dressed in her usual jeans and sweater, she added a quick slick of lipstick, tossed the dog a biscuit, and left the house. First stop on Tuesday was always the town hall, where she picked up the meeting schedule for the upcoming week. She always made a point of chatting up the girls in the town clerk's office, often picking up a lead on a story. This week, however, there was an awkward silence when she presented herself at the clerk's window.

"What's up?" she asked, with a bright smile.

"Uh, nothing, Lucy," the clerk's assistant, Andrea, replied. She was a chubby girl in her twenties, with thick brown hair pulled back into a frizzy ponytail.

"It's like somebody died in here," Lucy joked.

"No. We're all fine," Andrea said, handing her the meeting schedule. "Do you need anything else?"

Lucy glanced at the list, which included the usual selectmen's and FinCom meetings, as well as the Planning Committee and Conservation Committee. "Looks like a busy week," she said, hoping to get some sort of conversation going.

"If that's all, I have to get back to work," Andrea said.

"Of course," Lucy said, admitting defeat. Her reporter's nose told her something was definitely going on, something that nobody wanted her to find out about. There were no cheerful greetings, no hellos or good-byes as she passed the various town offices. Instead, heads were quickly turned as soon as she was spotted. She was beginning to wonder if she had the plague or something, when she bumped into Barney Culpepper at the entrance.

"Hey, Lucy!" At least he greeted her warmly.

"Hi, Barney. How's it going?"

"Can't complain," he said, taking off his official blue police winter cap, with the fur-lined ear flaps.

"Do you know what's going on?" she asked. "I got a really odd reception in there this morning."

He pulled her aside, away from the glass doors where they were clearly on view, into a sheltered alcove where a table was loaded with free information booklets on subjects such as preventing forest fires and how to obtain fishing licenses. "Don't say you heard it from me. . . ." he began.

"Of course not."

"The town employees are planning to stage a demonstration at the FinCom meeting Wednesday night. They're going to demand reinstatement of hours and benefits."

"Great," Lucy said. "I'm all for that. Why the attitude?"

"Because of Bill," Barney said. "He's on the committee. . . ."

". . . and I'm his wife," Lucy said, finishing the sentence.

"Yeah. I think they just feel awkward about it."

"Well, they shouldn't," Lucy said. "I'm on their side."

"But nobody knows how Bill's gonna vote," Barney said.

"Not even me," Lucy admitted. "It's going to be an interesting meeting."

"See you there," said Barney, with a wink.

Tuesdays were always busy at the *Pennysaver*, as they all worked to meet the noon Wednesday deadline, and for once Lucy was grateful for the constant pressure that kept her mind from obsessing about Sara. It was only when she left the office that she found herself brooding, worrying about where and with whom Sara would be spending the night.

Dinner was a quiet affair, with just the three of them gathered over tuna casserole at the kitchen table. Lucy was trying to think of a tactful way to warn Bill about the town employee's plans to demonstrate at the Fin-Com meeting when Zoe broke the silence.

"This is weird," Zoe declared. "I always wished I was an only child but now I don't like it."

"Why don't you like it?" Bill asked, helping himself to salad.

"Nowhere to hide," Zoe said, digging into the casserole. "Besides, I always come out looking pretty good in comparison to the others."

"You're just younger," Lucy said. "You haven't had a chance to get into trouble."

"But now . . ." Zoe began.

"Yes?" Lucy and Bill chorused, swiveling their heads to stare at their daughter.

Her reaction was instantaneous. "See!" she retorted, and they all laughed.

"You can consolidate your favored child status by doing the dishes," Lucy said. "I've got a rehearsal."

"Lucky me," Zoe moaned, but when they'd finished eating she got up and cleared the table without further protest. The leftovers had been wrapped and put away and the dishwasher was humming when Lucy left the house.

The night was cold and crisp and moonlight reflected off the snow that filled the woods and yards alongside the road. The little cluster of houses on Prudence Path were bright with Christmas lights, and the neighborhood looked like a picture on a Christmas card. Farther on, Lucy passed the turn to Shore Road and resolutely drove past, resisting the tug that drew her to Sara.

After rehearsal, Lucy stopped at the IGA to pick up a gallon of milk and some eggs for breakfast. The store was brightly lit but only a few cars were in the parking lot, including the Cunninghams aged Corolla. Lucy saw them in the cereal aisle as she hurried back to the dairy counter, which was located along the rear wall of the store, and attempted to avoid them by returning through the canned goods. She knew she was being a coward but she was tired. She'd had an emotionally exhausting day and she didn't feel up to coping with their difficult situation.

Her strategy didn't work, however, as she encountered Zach and Lexie at the checkout counter. Dot had added up their order and Lexie was handing over their SNAP benefit card when Lucy got in line behind them.

"Okay," Dot said. "That brings it down to twelve forty-nine, for the pet food."

Zach pulled out his wallet and discovered he only had nine dollars. "What have you got, Lexie?"

Lexie found she had two dollars and twenty-seven cents.

Zach sighed. "I'll take it back and get the smaller bag," he said, picking up the twenty-pound bag of dog chow.

"Don't bother," Lucy said, handing Zach a five-dollar bill. She didn't care if he paid it back but she knew Zach was proud, so she added, "Catch me later, when you've got it."

"Thanks," Zach said, as Dot gave him the change. He turned to Lucy with a serious expression. "I will pay you back."

"I wouldn't hold your breath," a male voice advised, and Lucy turned to see Ben Scribner standing in line behind her, holding a can of store-brand coffee. "Trust me. You can't count on folks who get government handouts and still can't make ends meet."

Suddenly, Lexie whirled around, her face distorted as she struggled with tears. "Who are you to criticize us?" she demanded. "You're a greedy, horrible, nasty, selfish man! You wreck people's lives! You should rot in hell—and I know you will!"

Embarrassed, Zach attempted to quiet his wife. "She doesn't mean it. She's just upset," he said. "Our daughter's in the hospital—she's very sick."

Much to Lucy's amazement, Ben Scribner's features seemed to soften. "Your little girl is sick? How old is she?"

"She's seven, not that you care," Lexie snapped. Her hair, which needed a wash, was pulled back into a ponytail. She wasn't wearing any makeup, not even lipstick on her thin, chapped lips. Her skin was pasty from being indoors too much and stretched so tight over her bones that Lucy thought it might crack.

"Her name's Angie," Zach said.

"And what's the problem?" Scribner asked.

"Juvenile polycystic kidney disease." Lexie hissed out the words.

"And can't the doctors do anything?"

"She needs a kidney transplant, but we're running out of time," Zach said.

"What do you mean?" Scribner asked.

"If she doesn't get it soon," Lexie said in a flat tone, "she's going to die."

Scribner looked astonished, as if the idea that a child could die had never occurred to him.

"So you can take our house if you want. I really don't

care, because Angie won't be there. It won't be our home, not without Angie." Lexie turned to Lucy. "Thanks for the loan. We'll pay you back next week," she said.

"Let me know if there's anything else I can do," Lucy said.

Lexie nodded and started to go, then suddenly whirled around and spat in Scribner's face, before running out of the store.

Dot reached under the counter for a roll of paper towels, but Lucy thought she took an awfully long time unrolling a few sheets and handing them to Scribner, so he could wipe the saliva off his face. It was as if she wanted to give him plenty of time to realize what had happened, and to consider what Lexie thought of him.

Chapter Seventeen

The big hand on the clock in the *Pennysaver* office was jerking its way to the twelve on Wednesday morning when Lucy hit the final period and sent Ted her last story, an account of the Planning Committee meeting, when the little bell on the door jangled and Rachel walked in.

"Hi," Lucy said, greeting her with a smile. Phyllis and Ted merely waved, being busy with last minute tasks.

"Is this a bad time?" Rachel asked. She looked frazzled, with dark circles under her eyes. Strands of long dark hair had escaped from her tortoiseshell clip and she kept tucking them behind her ears. When she unbuttoned her coat, Lucy saw she'd topped an unbecoming maroon turtleneck with a ratty old brown sweater, obviously the first things that came to hand.

"No, I'm done, unless Ted finds fault with my five inches on the Planning Committee."

"You're done," Ted said. "I don't think I've got room for it this week."

"I hate it when this happens," Lucy complained. "My precious prose, discarded on the scrap heap of journalism." She was hoping to get a smile from Rachel, but didn't succeed.

"I was just wondering, well, if maybe you could help me this afternoon," Rachel said, sounding as if she didn't really think Lucy would.

Lucy, however, wasn't about to turn her down. She wanted to find out what was causing her friend to be so unhappy. "Absolutely," she said. "What can I do?"

"Miss T and I are going to go over the costumes one last time and we could use another pair of hands. Are you sure you don't mind?" Rachel asked. "I mean, with Christmas and all you must have a lot to do."

"Nothing that can't wait," Lucy said, reaching for her purse.

"It seems an awful lot to ask," Rachel continued in a doubtful tone.

Lucy zipped up her parka and put an arm around Rachel's shoulders. "Look, let's get some coffee and a bite to eat, maybe an early lunch, and we'll take it from there."

At Jake's, Lucy ordered a BLT and a cola. Rachel got a bowl of chowder, which she stirred from time to time with her spoon but didn't eat. "What's going on?" Lucy asked, talking with her mouth full of crunchy toast.

Rachel's expression was bleak. "I don't know. I just can't seem to pull myself together."

"Maybe you've just taken on too much," Lucy said.

"That's what Bob says."

"So things are okay with you and Bob?" Lucy asked.

Rachel suddenly looked anxious. "What have you heard?"

"Nothing," Lucy said, quick to reassure her. "Nothing at all."

Rachel narrowed her eyes. "Sometimes I wish that scenery had done a little more damage to Florence."

Lucy smiled. "Bob's not the sort to be unfaithful."

"Florence doesn't seem to realize that," Rachel said. "She keeps calling and popping up. You've seen how she won't leave him alone at rehearsals."

"I've also seen how Bob brushes her off."

"She's like dog hair. No matter how much you brush her off there's always more."

Lucy laughed, relieved that Rachel hadn't entirely lost her sense of humor.

"The show's going well," Lucy said. "Isn't it?"

"It's coming together," Rachel admitted. "I asked Bill to stop by and check the scenery." She spooned up some chowder. "I hope you don't mind."

"Why would I mind?" Lucy asked, popping the last bit of BLT in her mouth.

"Well, I don't want you to think I'm after your husband or anything."

Lucy coughed and sputtered, choking and reaching for her drink. "Never crossed my mind," she finally said.

Rachel drove them both to Miss Tilley's little Cape house, which was decorated in the spirit of the season with a swag of greens tied with a red ribbon on the front door. Inside, Miss Tilley's small tabletop tree was decorated with antique kugels from Germany, which Lucy happened to know were worth quite a lot of money.

"Your tree is beautiful," Lucy said, examining the handblown ornaments.

"I remember those ornaments from my childhood." Miss Tilley was dressed as usual in a neat twin set and tweed skirt. Her white hair made a curly aureole around her pink-cheeked face. "I wasn't allowed to touch them."

"Is this tree fake?" Lucy asked, touching the plastic needles.

"Much safer for the ornaments," Miss Tilley said, pleased as punch to show that she wasn't stuck in the past. "And you can keep it up as long as you like—it doesn't drop its needles."

"But you don't get the piney scent," Lucy said, as Rachel helped the old woman into her broadcloth coat. She offered her arm to Miss Tilley when they trooped out to Rachel's car, since the walk was a bit slippery, but Miss Tilley refused it in a show of independence. She did the same when they arrived at the church, even sliding a bit on an icy patch as if she were ice skating. Lucy and Rachel exchanged a disapproving glance, as if their aged friend was instead a stubborn toddler.

Once inside, Rachel led them to a corner in the basement hall, where the costumes were hanging on a portable rack. They were stiff and dusty, so they shook them out, and checked that the buttons and zippers were all in working order and added labels identifying each one. A couple of pairs of trousers needed their length adjusted and Lucy busied herself with needle and thread. Miss Tilley brushed the top hats worn by the male characters, and Rachel let out the bodice of Marge Culpepper's costume, which was too tight.

"How are your children, Lucy?" Miss Tilley asked. "Is Elizabeth still working at that hotel in Florida?"

"She is, and she has to work Christmas Day but she's coming the day after."

"Boxing Day," Miss Tilley said. "In Dickens's day

rich folk boxed up their old clothes and gave them to their servants on Boxing Day."

"We could use a little more of that spirit these days," Rachel said. "Ticket sales are behind last year's."

"It's the economy," Lucy said. "People are hurting."

"Not everyone is hurting," Miss Tilley sniffed.

"Now you sound like Sara," Lucy said. "She's joined the social action group at Winchester College."

"Good for her," Miss Tilley said. "I like a girl who acts on her convictions."

"I'm not sure whether it's convictions or simple teenage rebellion," Lucy said. "She's left home and is squatting in a foreclosed house on Shore Road."

Rachel paused, seam ripper in hand, a horrified expression on her face. "I'm so sorry, Lucy. Here I was going on about my problems when you must be sick with worry."

"To tell the truth, I'm past worry. Now I'm mostly annoyed."

"But what if she gets arrested?" Rachel asked.

"I hope she does," Lucy declared. "It will teach her a lesson."

"Or confirm her in her beliefs," Miss Tilley said, holding Scrooge's top hat up to the light. "Such a silly fashion," she said. "Isn't it odd what people will wear?"

"Sure is," Bill said. His arrival let in a gust of chilly air. "You wouldn't catch me wearing a hat like that."

"You'd look quite handsome," Miss Tilley said, winking at him.

"Want to try it on?" Lucy teased.

"No way!" Bill hoisted the toolbox he was carrying. "Now what exactly do you want me to do?" he asked Rachel.

"You know how the scenery fell on Florence. I just want to make sure it doesn't happen again. I don't want any more accidents, especially during the performance."

Bill went up on stage, flipping the lights on, and disappeared behind the partly painted flats. He was only gone a moment or two before he returned. "Looks fine to me," he said, with a shrug. "It's been bolted together and there are braces on the side panels that weren't there before. It's not going to fall."

"Al must have worked on it since the accident," Lucy said.

"Yeah," Bill said. "Those struts weren't there before, and the sections weren't bolted together. It's much safer now."

"But it wasn't safe before?" Lucy asked.

"It wasn't finished," Bill said. "It was a temporary setup."

Lucy was thoughtful. "So you're saying those flats fell because they weren't constructed properly?"

"That's the only way it could've happened," Bill said. "I wouldn't have left them like that but different people do things different ways."

"It does seem terribly careless," Miss Tilley said.

"I'm not sure careless is the word," Lucy said, remembering Florence saying she heard a noise and felt a draft just before the scenery fell, and her sense that she hadn't been alone.

Bill gave her a sharp look. "Anybody can make a mistake," he said, but she knew what he really meant. He was warning her not to poke her nose into matters that didn't concern her.

That evening she found herself accompanying Bill to the Finance Committee meeting. From what Barney had told her about the town employees it was going to be a tense affair and she wanted to give Bill a heads up. She offered him a little advice as they drove into town.

"I've heard rumors that the town employees are going to show up in force tonight, demanding their old hours and benefits," she said. "You're going to need to keep a cool head and remember it's not about you. You didn't vote to make the cuts."

"I think I can handle whatever happens," Bill said, in a *mind-your-own-business* tone of voice.

I sure hope so, Lucy thought, but didn't say it out loud. She was pretty sure Bill didn't have a clue about the firestorm he was walking into. In fact, the meeting room was packed with town employees and members of the Winchester Social Action Committee when they arrived. Seth Lesinski and his cohorts were seated together on one side of the aisle, while town employees including Harry Crawford, Phil Watkins, and Nelson Macmillan were scattered among the usual concerned citizens on the other.

Lucy took her usual seat near the front of the room and Bill joined the other board members at the long table facing the audience, seating himself behind his shiny new nameplate. At seven o'clock precisely chairman Gene Hawthorne called the meeting to order and, as always, opened the public comment portion of the meeting.

Seth Lesinski immediately jumped to his feet. "I'm here tonight with members—" he began, only to be silenced by Hawthorne.

"It's usual to wait to be recognized by the chair before speaking," he said.

"Sorry," Seth said. "Am I recognized?"

"Go ahead," said Hawthorne, looking annoyed.

"Now that I've been *officially* recognized," Seth began with a smirk, "I'm here to say that I represent the Social Action Committee at Winchester College. Today the committee voted to demand complete and full restitution to the Tinker's Cove town employees' hours, wages, and benefits, and also to demand that town officials immediately demand that Downeast Mortgage cease and desist from foreclosing on delinquent mortgage holders."

This brief speech was well received by most audience members, who clapped and cheered.

Gene Hawthorne once again called for order. "Thank you for your input," he said, when the group finally quieted down. "I would like to point out, however, that tonight's meeting will be limited to discussion and action on the items listed on the previously posted agenda."

This announcement was met with a rumble of disapproval from the audience.

"Well, how do we get on the agenda?" Seth demanded.

"As I mentioned earlier, you need to be recognized by the chair before speaking," said Hawthorne, with a sigh.

Lesinski rolled his eyes and raised his hand.

"Mr. Lesinski," Hawthorne said. "Go ahead."

"I guess this is a point of order," Seth said in a challenging tone of voice. "How exactly does a concerned citizen place an item on the agenda?"

"You contact the committee secretary, Mrs. Mahoney, and she will take it from there. The agenda is posted one week prior to the meeting."

"May I ask another question?" Seth asked. He was bouncing on the balls of his feet.

"You may."

"In effect, that means that at a minimum the committee cannot act on reinstating hours and benefits before next week, which takes us right up to Christmas, right?"

"Actually a bit longer, because we have to vote to include an item on the agenda," Hawthorne said. "And we won't meet again until after Christmas."

"May I speak again?" Seth asked, bouncing a bit faster.

"You may."

"Can you consider taking that vote tonight, at this meeting?"

Hawthorne checked with the other committee members, who indicated they were open to the suggestion.

Jerry Taubert, however, had a cautionary bit of information. "I don't mind voting to include it in a future agenda, but it's really pointless. I'm all for reinstating hours and wages, but the fact is that there simply isn't enough cash on hand in the town account."

"He's right," Bill said. "I've been going over the accounts and there's not much wiggle room, that's for sure. Tax receipts are down and so is state aid."

"And furthermore," Frankie added, "on the other matter, I don't believe the town actually has the authority to tell Downeast Mortgage to stop foreclosures. That's something the town counsel would have to look into."

Hearing this, the crowd became extremely restive. "Well, that's what we pay him for," someone yelled. Harry Crawford and several other men were on their feet, demanding a vote.

"Do I have a motion?" Hawthorne asked, banging his gavel.

Pam raised her hand, moving that Lesinski's demands be placed on the agenda for the next meeting, which was scheduled to take place early in January, after the usual Christmas break. Frankie seconded it and Hawthorne called for discussion, recognizing Jerry Taubert.

"This is a waste of time," he said, getting a smattering of boos. "Our hands are tied. We don't have the money to reinstate town employees. We'd have to raise taxes and we can't do that without a town meeting vote."

"Hold a special town meeting!" Phil Watkins yelled, eliciting cheers from the citizenry.

"Order! Order!" demanded Hawthorne, banging his gavel. When the crowd quieted down he recognized Bill. Lucy shifted uneasily in her seat.

"As for the demand that the town order Downeast Mortgage to stop foreclosures," said Bill, "I have to point out that there is simply no way we can do that. That is simply a matter of contractual obligations between private parties, and the town has no standing whatsoever in the . . ."

The crowd certainly didn't like hearing this, especially not the SAC kids, who were muttering and booing. Lucy discovered she was holding her breath. She was so tense that her stomach hurt. It was killing her to sit there when she wanted to leap to Bill's defense.

Gene Hawthorne called for order, once again, this time warning that he would have the room cleared unless the crowd observed the proper decorum. Receiving grudging acquiescence, he called for a vote on the motion. "All in favor," he said, and the room fell silent as Frankie and Pam raised their hands.

"Against?" The three men on the committee raised their hands, and the audience immediately erupted with a unified roar.

In a matter of seconds everyone was on their feet. Cardboard coffee cups, balled up wads of paper, even chairs were hurled into the air. The committee members ducked behind their table. Lucy herself adopted a crash position, curling up and placing her arms above her head. Barney Culpepper was blowing his whistle, the meeting room doors were thrown open, and the Tinker's Cove Police Department, all seven officers who had been positioned outside, poured into the room. Seeing the officers in blue, the Winchester group bolted en masse for a side exit. Local folk were more easily subdued, but Harry Crawford did attempt to punch Officer Todd Kirwan. Kirwan avoided the punch and Barney applied the handcuffs, hustling Crawford out of the building.

"Meeting adjourned," Hawthorne declared, wiping his brow with a handkerchief, and the shaken committee members began gathering up their papers and belongings.

Hildy, the freelancer Ted had asked to cover the meeting, was already interviewing Hawthorne. "What's your reaction to tonight's events?" she was asking, as Lucy joined Bill, who was gathering up his papers.

Hawthorne shook his head. "We can't have this sort of thing," he said. "In future, we will have strict security at our meetings. The committee can't work under these conditions, and I want to say that these committee members are struggling with a very difficult fiscal situation and doing their very best to make responsible decisions."

Bill nodded in agreement. "It's very different to be sitting on this side of the table," he said. "We can't be influenced by an unruly mob." Then he took Lucy's arm and they made their way through the overturned chairs and litter to the door.

"Well, don't say I didn't warn you," she said.

"Bunch of hooligans," Bill muttered.

"Those hooligans include your daughter," Lucy said.

"She wasn't here tonight," Bill observed. "At least I didn't see her."

"No, she was probably back at the squat, building bombs."

"Don't joke about it," Bill said sternly, as they climbed into the pickup. "It's not funny."

"I wasn't joking," Lucy said. "There are going to be repercussions, and if I were you, I'd be very careful for the next few days."

"Don't be ridiculous." Bill shifted into reverse and backed out of his parking spot. "Everybody loves me."

"Not anymore," Lucy said.

Chapter Eighteen

Thursday morning, Lucy was lingering in bed with a cup of coffee, watching a morning news show on the old TV that had migrated upstairs when they bought a new flat screen for the family room. The weather reporter was predicting more stormy weather when Bill stomped up the stairs and blew into their bedroom.

"Somebody slashed my tires!" he exclaimed. His tone of voice left no doubt that he was really upset. Also shocked, angry, and indignant. "Can you believe it?"

"Actually, I can," Lucy said, recalling that she had predicted trouble after the contentious FinCom meeting.

He sat on the edge of the bed. "Who would do such a thing?"

"Somebody who's mad at you," Lucy said.

"Because of my vote?"

"Probably." Lucy had a few ideas on the subject. "Or to make a point."

"You know how much this is gonna cost us?" Bill asked. "And not just cash. Time, too. I'm gonna lose an entire day of work, getting new tires."

"You should report it to the police," Lucy said. "It's not just property damage. You're a public official. I'm pretty sure that attempting to intimidate a public official is a crime."

"Somehow I don't think I'm going to get much sympathy from the police department," Bill said. "They're town employees, too."

"True," Lucy said, patting his knee. "And to think, everyone used to love you."

Bill scowled and scratched his beard, now mixed with gray. "At least I know I can count on you not to throw my own words back at me."

"I would never do that," Lucy said, throwing the covers back and getting up. As she stood Bill grabbed her by the hips and pulled her down; she laughed as she rolled back on the bed. "I can't, Bill, I can't. I've got breakfast with the girls in half an hour."

"You're going to be late," Bill said, kissing her and groping for the buttons on her pajamas.

When she was in the car, on her way to Jake's, Lucy suddenly changed her mind about meeting her friends for breakfast. The four friends had agreed early on that their Thursday morning breakfasts were such an important commitment that only serious illness or death counted as legitimate excuses for breaking the date. This morning, however, Lucy found herself calling Sue and begging off. There was something she wanted to do, something that wouldn't wait.

"Well, this is a fine howdy do," Sue said, sounding annoyed. "Rachel's already called and said she's simply got too much to do to make it."

"Oh." Lucy felt a twinge of guilt but brushed it aside. "I hope this isn't a trend."

"Well, it is only a few days till Christmas." Sue sighed. "Pam called last night and said she could only stay for half an hour. She wants to get to an early bird sale at the outlet mall."

Lucy knew that Sue was a dedicated shopper. "Why don't you go with her?" she suggested.

"I think I will," Sue said. "But no excuses next week, right?"

"No excuses," Lucy promised, closing her flip phone and making the turn onto Shore Road.

Glancing out over the ocean, Lucy saw the sky was full of thick gray clouds, hanging low. The water itself was slate gray and choppy. It was the sort of scene that made you fear for anyone out on the sea and, living on the coast, Lucy knew there were plenty of fishermen, coast guardsmen, sailors, and merchant seamen who braved the waves every day. Lucy thought of the plaques on the walls of the Community Church, engraved with the names of those who had gone to sea and never returned: Isaiah Walker, who fell overboard in pursuit of a whale, Ephraim Snodgrass, who contracted yellow fever en route to Manila, and Horace Sanford, USN, whose troop ship was torpedoed by a German U-boat. She shivered, thinking of those poor souls, and the many others who met their fate in the cold depths of the North Atlantic.

Turning into the driveway at the squat, she saw, as before, it was filled with numerous cars. She marched resolutely up to the porch, pushed open the unlocked door and stepped inside, where she was immediately met by Seth Lesinski.

"Here for a reaction to the FinCom meeting?" he asked, with a wide grin. He was holding a big mug of tea in one hand, a laptop computer in the other, and seemed terribly pleased with himself.

"Not exactly," Lucy said, following him into the library, away from other members of the group who were gathering in the living room.

Seth seated himself at a card table and opened the computer, then leaned back in his chair and took a long drink of tea. "So what can I do for you?" he asked.

"You can stop this campaign of intimidation, that's what you can do," Lucy said, picking up steam.

"I'd call it information, not intimidation," he said.

"My husband's tires were slashed last night," Lucy said in an accusatory tone, "and I think you know all about it."

Seth's eyebrows rose. "I don't."

"I don't believe you," Lucy replied. "And I wouldn't be the least bit surprised to learn you were behind the bombing that killed Jake Marlowe."

"That's crazy," Seth said, looking both shocked and troubled. "How could you ever think I wanted to kill that pathetic old man?"

"I don't think you intended to kill him. I think you meant to frighten him but things went wrong. You're a combat veteran—you know all about guns and explosives. . . ." Lucy said, only to be interrupted.

"Yeah, I know about explosives, but from the wrong end. I've lost good friends, seen them literally ripped apart by IEDs. I would never . . . I'm a patriot, no matter what you might think. I love this country and that's why I'm doing what I'm doing. I'm trying to save it from the greedy bastards who are sucking it dry."

Lucy felt herself falling under his sway. She was almost convinced, actually feeling rather ashamed of her suspicions, when she caught herself. He was clever, she reminded herself, a master manipulator who had seduced her daughter mentally, if not physically. Sara! She suddenly had an urgent, overwhelming need to contact her daughter. Where was Sara?

"Is my daughter here?" she asked in a no-nonsense tone.

"Sara?" he asked.

"Yes, Sara! You know, Sara!"

He shook his head. "I haven't seen her this morning."

And I hope you never see her again, Lucy thought, turning on her heel and heading for the door. Glancing over her shoulder, she caught a glimpse of his computer screen: it pictured a classic comic book bomb, a sinister black globe with a sizzling wick, in front of a waving American flag, and the words *Extremism in the defense of liberty is no vice!*

Her eyes widened and she suddenly felt justified. So much for Seth Lesinski and his protestations of patriotism, his denial of violent tactics! The man was a domestic terrorist and he was seducing decent kids with social consciences to join him. He had to be stopped, she fumed, yanking the car door open and jumping inside. She was going to go straight to the police, she decided. This had gone far enough. It was time for the grown-ups to take charge.

When she marched into Police Chief Jim Kirwan's office, she was surprised to see that Ben Scribner was already there.

"That house belongs to Downeast Mortgage and I demand police action!" he was saying. "Those kids have moved in like they own the place. The utilities are off, you know. No water, no power, no heat. You can only imagine what's going on, the damage they're causing."

"It's worse than that," Lucy said, eager to join the discussion. "They've slashed Bill's tires, and they've got bombs on their computers. . . ."

Both Scribner and Kirwan looked at her. "Bombs?" the chief repeated.

"Bombs!" Lucy declared.

"What's this about tires?"

"All four tires on Bill's truck were slashed this morning," Lucy said. "And you heard Seth Lesinski at the meeting last night, all but predicting violence if their demands weren't met."

"That's not proof," the chief said.

"It's proof enough for me!" Scribner declared. "It's my property and I demand action! I'm a taxpayer, probably the town's biggest taxpayer, and I want those hooligans out of there by the end of the day!"

The chief scowled in concentration, considering his course of action. Finally, he nodded. "Okay," he said, and reached for the phone.

Lucy enjoyed a few moments of self-righteous satisfaction as she made her way to the *Pennysaver* office, congratulating herself that she'd actually managed to help convince the chief to take the correct action. It wasn't until she was walking into the office that it occurred to her to wonder at the strange turn of events that had caused her own interests to align with those of Ben Scribner. That was when she began to doubt she'd done the right thing, but by then it was too late. The police scanner was already buzzing as forces assembled and prepared to raid the squat.

Lucy covered it, of course, standing by the side of the road and snapping photos as uniformed SWAT team members from the state police deployed, accompanied by local officers, and stormed the shingled cottage. The squatters were brought out with their hands fastened behind their backs in plastic snap ties, their coats over their shoulders, and loaded into a school bus. Lucy was clicking away when Sara's face appeared on the digital video screen and she had the sickening realization that her daughter would probably never forgive her.

Once the house was emptied of squatters a team of crime scene investigators went to work, and Lucy also photographed them removing boxes and bags of material. When she asked if they had found evidence of domestic terrorism all she got was a stern "No comment."

Following up at the police station, Kirwan would only say that "the material taken from the squat will be analyzed for evidence of domestic terrorism." For the moment the squatters would be charged with trespassing and the arraignments were under way in Gilead. Lucy raced to the courthouse in the county seat, arriving just in time to produce bail for Sara.

Sara, much to her mother's irritation, did not express gratitude for the hundred dollars in cash that Lucy had extracted from the conveniently located ATM in the courthouse lobby. "I missed a poli sci quiz, 'cause of those cops!" Sara fumed. "And I studied and everything."

"I'm sure you can make it up. Maybe even get extra credit for getting arrested," Lucy said. "You got first-hand experience of the justice system. You should offer to write a paper for extra credit."

Sara narrowed her eyes. "Don't be all snarky, Mom."

"I'm not. I'm serious," Lucy said.

"The judge was horrible. He acted like we were criminals or something."

"You broke the law," Lucy reminded her. "Trespassing is a crime, and after last night's meeting, they're going to suspect the group of doing more than just squatting. You know your father's tires were slashed? Do you know anything about that?"

"No. Of course not. Seth wouldn't have anything to do with violence. He said he saw it firsthand in Iraq and Afghanistan and it's made him a committed pacifist. He believes in passive resistance. When the cops came he told us to go limp and let them arrest us, not to struggle or anything." Sara turned her head and stared out the window of the car, apparently fascinated by the snowy fields and bare trees along the road. "It was you!" she suddenly declared, whirling around to accuse her mother. "You're the one who got the cops to raid the squat!"

"Not really," Lucy said. "I reported the tire-slashing— of course I did. Your dad is a public official and this is intimidation. It's illegal, and it was my duty to report it." She paused, but Sara's expression remained angry and accusatory. "I think it was really Ben Scribner who convinced the chief. He demanded action and he's got friends in high places. I don't think the chief had any alternative, really. It was a question of property rights."

"Private property is theft," Sara declared.

"Well, then I guess you won't mind sharing your Uggs with Zoe and letting her wear them every other day, will you?"

Sara didn't have an answer for that, so she turned her head once again and watched the scenery roll by.

Lucy also was silent, wondering if her suspicions about Seth Lesinski were indeed correct. Sara was young and easily influenced, but she knew that her daughter was really a good person at heart. She wouldn't condone violence—she wouldn't have anything to do with it, of that Lucy was convinced. Maybe Sara was right about Seth Lesinski, and maybe she herself was wrong. But if that was so, who had sent the bomb? And did the same person slash Bill's tires? Were they going to find a brightly wrapped bomb in their mailbox, too?

That night was the dress rehearsal, the final run-through before the weekend performances. Florence had finished painting the scenery, which was still wet, in fact, and Rachel warned everyone to keep clear of it for fear of staining their costumes. Even so, Lucy found the addition of the subtly designed scenery and costumes transformed the show and made it much more believable. Now, Bob wasn't Bob reciting odd, old-fashioned language, he was Scrooge, complete with mutton-chop whiskers, an enormous pocket watch with a massive gold chain and fob, and a high top hat. And she found it easier to believe herself in the role of Mrs. Cratchit, thanks to the long, full-skirted dress and lace-trimmed mobcap.

Lucy knew she was not really much of an actor, but when she played the Christmas Yet to Come scene in which Tiny Tim is predicted to have died, she found tears welling in her eyes. Her voice broke as she gazed at his crutch leaning on the wall, no longer needed, and recalled how Bob Cratchit had found his crippled son "very light indeed" when he carried him on his shoulders.

Rachel gave her a big thumbs-up when she exited the stage, but her thoughts had strayed from Victorian England to the present. It was the possibility that Tiny Tim might die that finally melted Scrooge's hard heart, and Lucy wondered if learning that Angie Cunningham was actually in danger of dying might work in some way to soften Ben Scribner's heart. Or not, she thought, remembering how adamantly he'd insisted that the police clear his property of squatters.

Tragic situations had effects that were hard to predict. She thought of Al Roberts's surprising, angry reaction when the cast members had offered to help him. If he'd been in his right mind, he would have taken her up on her offer and borrowed her car. But his emotions got in the way. Lucy suspected his anger about Angie's situation had grown until it colored everything, including the foreclosure. Did he believe that Scribner was the author of all the family's problems, and had he attempted to get back at Scribner by rigging the scenery to fall on his niece, Florence? Al had walked over to the caroling with her and Bob and Rachel, but he could have left them and gone back to the church hall. She didn't remember seeing him among the crowd gathered around the bonfire, singing carols.

She was pulled back to the present when Rachel announced it was time to run through the curtain call, which she predicted would be a standing ovation, and all thoughts of Ben Scribner and Al Roberts and Angie disappeared in the euphoria of the moment. Rachel was over the top, once everyone was on stage, holding hands and bowing together. She clapped and bravoed and congratulated them all, assuring them that the show would be a terrific success.

Lucy was practically floating as she made her way to the Sunday School classroom that was serving as the women's dressing room, when she passed Bob in the hallway. He was talking on his cell phone, apparently making an appointment with a client who wanted his will written.

"Okay, Al," he was saying. "I can do it tomorrow, but I don't see what the rush is." Then there was silence, while Bob was listening and nodding. "Okay, we'll make it bright and early—nine o'clock suit you?" Then he ended the call, but remained in the hallway, obviously troubled.

"Is something the matter?" Lucy asked.

"Oh, Lucy," he said, looking up and smiling at her. "Great job tonight."

Lucy shook her head. "You're the star of the show; you were fabulous. I had no idea you had such a mean streak. Who knew that there's a nasty old miser hiding somewhere inside nice generous Bob Goodman?"

Bob chuckled. "It's just acting, I'm happy to say."

"Oh, right," Lucy said, teasing him.

"How's Bill doing?" he asked. "I heard there was quite a kerfuffle at the FinCom meeting last night."

"Not too good," Lucy said. "Somebody slashed the tires on his truck."

Bob's eyebrows rose in shock. "I know the town employees are angry about the cuts, but I didn't think they'd do anything like that."

"Funny," Lucy said. "My first thought was that it was the students, that group led by Seth Lesinski. Kids can be really irresponsible and do crazy stuff."

"Maybe," Bob admitted. "But the town employees have really been hurt by the cuts. Here's just one example. This guy, I'm not gonna mention any names, worked for years and rose through the ranks until he was head of his department. Then he had some health problems and had to take early retirement. He got what probably seemed like a big payout at the time but now isn't so much. He's in real financial trouble. . . ."

Hearing Rachel's voice, calling him for a photo, Bob paused.

"Listen, forget I said that. I shouldn't talk about my clients—" He stopped abruptly. "I'm making it worse, aren't I?"

"Forget it," Lucy said, waving her hand. "I didn't hear a word of it."

Chapter Nineteen

On Friday morning Lucy woke with an odd mixture of dread and excitement—butterflies were definitely fluttering in her tummy. The show was hours away but she knew she was going to be nervously anticipating the opening curtain all day. What if she forgot her lines? What if she suddenly went blank? What then? A million things could go wrong in a stage show, which depended on the perfectly timed efforts of everyone involved, not only the actors but all the behind-the-scenes workers, too. All she could do was keep repeating her lines and hope that everybody else was focused on the show, too.

But first she had a long day to get through. Friday was generally a slow day at the *Pennysaver,* in which she developed a news budget, a list of stories for the next week's edition. She usually started by going through the press releases that had been sent to the paper, looking for possible story ideas. She also checked the town hall calendar of meetings, as well as the docket at the county courthouse. Then, when she'd put together a list of ideas, she checked with Ted, who nixed or approved her ideas and sometimes had a suggestion or two.

There was no rush to get to the office, but Lucy was full of nervous energy and found herself unlocking the door at just a few minutes past eight. Phyllis didn't come in until nine and Ted, being the boss, arrived whenever he felt like it, which was usually around ten-thirty on Fridays, sometimes later. Lucy considered making a pot of coffee and decided against it. Caffeine was the last thing she needed. Her nerves were all ajangle already. Skipping ahead to the next step in her Friday routine, she got the big accordion file of press releases and carried it to her desk, where she began to go through it. It was quite thin this close to Christmas, and nothing caught her interest. Her mind turned to what Bob had told her about one of his clients.

He hadn't given a name, but Lucy remembered writing a story a few years ago when Al Roberts retired, and she was pretty sure that he was the employee whom Bob was talking about. It had been the usual congratulatory fluff piece about an employee who had served the town for many years. In Al's case, he'd been with the highway department for some thirty years, ending his career as superintendent. Even so, thought Lucy, he was a young retiree, not yet sixty. Why, she wondered, had he stopped working at such a relatively young age? As superintendent, he didn't have to perform difficult physical labor. It was an office job, involving meetings and negotiations and scheduling, with occasional site visits to check on work in progress. He had been making good money, too, by local standards. Why did he give it all up? And why had he hired a lawyer?

Lucy suspected two possibilities: Al Roberts had been forced to take early retirement because of either a job performance matter or a health issue. Job performance was an area that nobody in town government liked to talk about, because it made employees and officials vulnerable to criticism from taxpayers. Lucy understood that it was simply unfair for a teacher, for example, to be subject to public scrutiny and criticism for a personal matter, perhaps needing extra sick days to care for an ailing relative. Lucy knew only too well how critical some taxpayers could be of town employees, always eager to claim the privilege because they were ultimately paying the employees' salaries. When it came to health issues and disability claims, especially disability claims, those were even more likely to unleash a torrent of angry outrage.

But as much as Lucy understood the need for town employees' job evaluations to remain confidential, she was often frustrated when she encountered this protective wall of silence. Not everything had to make it into print, but background knowledge was valuable to a reporter in that it gave greater understanding of issues and tensions affecting public policy. It helped to know that the superintendent of schools and the town treasurer absolutely loathed each other. If Lucy needed a comment from the town treasurer on a school budget matter, or vice versa, she knew she was likely to get an unprintable reply.

On the other hand, she admitted ruefully, sometimes she wanted to spice things up a bit. Then a call did the trick, with the addition of a few asterisks and exclamation points because the *Pennysaver* was decidedly a "family-friendly" publication.

This Al Roberts thing was none of her business, she reminded herself, but somehow she couldn't put it out of her mind. It sat there, nibbling away at her thoughts,

popping up when she tried to concentrate on the Girl
Scout carol sing at the old folks' home or the New
Year's Eve party at the VFW. Lucy knew perfectly well
that Roger Wilcox, the chairman of the Board of Selectmen, would insist on maintaining the confidentiality of
Roberts's records, and Bob Goodman would claim
client privilege, but she was also aware of the boxes of
town documents that Bill had stashed away in his office.
Those boxes were a treasure trove of information, but
she was forbidden from looking at them.

They were extremely tempting, but it would be a violation of journalistic ethics to even peek at them. Even
worse, a violation of marital ethics, because Bill was entitled to privacy. She wouldn't think of opening a letter
addressed to him, except for the bills, which were her
responsibility to pay. She would never open a personal
letter, like a birthday card or something like that. Never.

She could picture the boxes, however, the image quite
clear in her mind. They were beige with a brown stripe,
and the words *Documents* was printed on them. They
squatted there, in her imagination, and wouldn't leave.
It was like that second chocolate bar, a buy-one-get-one-
free offer, perhaps. You ate the first and saved the second for later, but you couldn't quite put it out of your
mind and you ended up eating it, too.

Lucy checked the clock on the office wall. It was
barely nine. Bill would be at his current job, a summer
cottage colony renovation, and Ted wasn't due anytime
soon. She was only after background information, she
told herself, pushing back her chair and reaching for her
coat. Deep background, that was all.

Even so, despite her efforts to rationalize away her
guilt, she had the uneasy sense that she was doing some-

thing wrong when she climbed the narrow stairs to Bill's attic office. Up there, under the sharply angled ceiling, he'd carved out a space for his desk and files. It was his haven, away from the family, and he'd decorated the walls with framed baseball cards from his boyhood collection and New England Patriots posters. Lucy ignored quarterback Tom Brady's rather disapproving gaze as she opened the first box, which contained computer printouts of the town budget from recent years. There was no way she could make head nor tail of that, she decided, replacing the lid.

The second box, however, was more interesting as it contained minutes of the FinCom's meetings, including those of executive sessions. Executive sessions were closed to the public and the press and usually concerned confidential personnel matters such as contract negotiations and disability payments. They had been filed neatly according to date and she soon found records of a discussion concerning Al Roberts's retirement.

According to the minutes, Roberts had requested early retirement on medical grounds, claiming injuries sustained some seventeen years earlier in a roads project. Roberts, who was then foreman of the town's road crew, had set a dynamite charge that exploded too soon and he was injured by flying debris. That injury, he claimed with the support of medical documentation, was now causing moderate to severe back pain that made it impossible for him to continue working as superintendent.

Jake Marlowe had questioned Roberts's claim, pointing out that the town had paid his medical expenses at the time of the accident. He also noted that when Roberts subsequently filed a lawsuit claiming disability, the committee offered him a lump-sum payment that he accepted, rather than taking the case to court. The amount, twenty-five thousand dollars, had probably seemed generous at the time but, Lucy thought, now seemed rather paltry. Marlowe didn't mince words, however, accusing Roberts of attempting to blackmail the committee with this new demand for early retirement. Instead, he suggested, the committee should simply refuse to renew his contract and look for a replacement. In other words, Marlowe had threatened to fire Roberts.

Wow, Lucy thought, sitting back on her heels. She had no idea this was going on. And to think she'd always found FinCom meetings to be boring. Actually, they were. All the exciting stuff took place in executive session.

Reading on, Lucy discovered that cooler heads had prevailed. Jerry Taubert had pointed out that granting early retirement would be far less costly than deciding the matter in court, and he for one thought Roberts had done a very good job as superintendent. Frankie and Pam had also voiced support for Roberts, leaving only Gene Hawthorne to side with Marlowe.

When it came to awarding Roberts's pension, however, Taubert switched sides. Roberts had wanted his pension to be calculated based on the years he would have worked to age sixty-five, but the committee voted to include only the years actually worked, although they did allow him to start collecting immediately.

The actual figures weren't mentioned in the minutes, however, and Lucy had to check those town budgets for the actual payroll figures. She flipped through quite a lot of pages of numbers and finally discovered that Al Roberts was getting $1,257 a month, but Frank Sullivan, the former building inspector who had retired at age sixty-five, was getting $1,979 a month. Lucy did a quick calculation and discovered that was a difference of more than $700 a month.

What did seven hundred dollars a month mean to a man like Al Roberts, Lucy wondered. The answer was clear: it was the difference between keeping up on his mortgage payments or losing his house to foreclosure. She knew he was an angry man and, she realized with a start, he did have some experience with explosives. The question was, she thought, whether he was content to vent his anger through the legal system, or whether he'd taken things further by sending a package bomb to Jake Marlowe. She knew he'd hired Bob, and she hoped that indicated he was content to work within the legal system, but thinking back to Bob's conversation with Roberts, she sensed that Roberts had been growing impatient.

Lucy realized her legs were cramping and she got to her feet, then bent over to stretch out her hamstrings. It wouldn't hurt, she thought, to go and talk to Al. Maybe she could do a feature story about how the recession was forcing many elders to take early retirement, and use Al's case as an example. Perhaps the FinCom would even revisit the issue and take another vote. Perhaps that would be enough to save his house from foreclosure—at the very least it would give him a bit more income with which to find another place to live.

Lucy drove slowly, not sure she was doing the right thing. Al Roberts had a bit of a temper. What if he turned on her? What if he didn't like her nosing around in his affairs? What if he thought she should mind her own business?

Turning down Bumps River Road, Lucy was struck once again by the obvious signs of poverty. Quite a few of the little houses were in disrepair; many sat in yards filled with discarded appliances and wrecked cars. When you were poor, she knew, you hated to let go of anything that might come in useful later. That wrecked car contained parts that could be used to repair another car. And that dryer that no longer ran? It cost money to leave it at the dump and maybe it could be used as a rabbit hutch? Or a food safe, especially in winter, when it could serve as a makeshift freezer. One man's trash was another's treasure, and that was nowhere truer than on Bumps River Road.

Al Roberts's little house, at the corner of Murtry Road, was neater than most and in fine repair. The roof was neatly shingled, and the porch contained only a couple of dark green Adirondack chairs. Lucy knocked on the door, and when there was no answer she cupped her hands around her eyes and peeked through the living room window. There was a plaid couch, a large picture of a stag hung above it, and a coffee table sat in the middle of the room on the braided rug. Squinting to see more clearly, she tried to make out the objects scattered on the coffee table, which appeared to be tools and wire and a broken cell phone.

What was he up to? she wondered, trying the door and finding it unlocked. Pushing it open, she called out a hello, and then his name. Her voice echoed through the empty rooms and, after hesitating a few moments, she stepped inside. Getting a closer look at the coffee table, she felt a rising sense of anxiety. This looked an awful lot like the makings of a bomb. She wasn't sure— maybe he'd just been trying to repair his cell phone, but who did that? You just took it back to the service provider and got a new one, didn't you? Noticing a neatly folded square of paper, she picked it up, discovering that her hands were shaking. Opening it, she gasped in shock as she read the neat, block-style print.

Sorry, Lexie, but it's better this way. You'll get the insurance money, and maybe there'll be enough left of me to save my kidneys. Love always, Dad.

Suddenly dizzy, Lucy sat down hard in an armchair and immediately began searching for her cell phone, frantically scrabbling through the contents of her handbag. When she finally retrieved it she hit 9-1-1 for the police department.

"What is your emergency?" the dispatcher asked—Dot Kirwan's daughter Krissy.

"A suicide bomber." Lucy's throat was tight; she could barely get the words out.

"Location?"

Lucy went blank. "Oh, golly, I don't know. I found a note." She considered the possibilities. "I bet he's going to Downeast Mortgage. He's going to blow the place up, and himself, too."

"Do you have a victim?"

"Not yet. You've got to hurry. Get there before he does it."

"Who? Who's the bomber?"

"Al Roberts." Lucy couldn't believe this. What was the problem? They had to get a squad car over to Downeast Mortgage, immediately. It was a matter of life and death.

"You think he's going to blow up Downeast Mortgage?" Krissy sounded doubtful.

"And himself. I found a suicide note."

"But no body?"

"No! But I'm pretty sure . . . it says something about insurance money and that he hopes there'll be *enough left* of him to donate his kidneys."

"I don't have an available unit," Krissy said. "They're all out at an accident on the interstate."

"Call mutual aid," Lucy snapped. The town's rescue services had agreements with neighboring towns to provide help in an emergency."

"I can only call mutual aid for an actual emergency," Krissy explained.

"But that will be too late!" Lucy tried not to yell.

"Look, I'll send a unit over to Downeast as soon as one's available. That's the best I can do. I'm sorry, but it's not like anybody's bleeding in the street."

"Not yet," Lucy said, flipping her phone shut and running out to her car. She repeated those words as she sped over the narrow, snow-banked roads to town. "Not yet, Lord, please, not yet. Not yet. Let me get there in time. Please. Not yet."

It was eerily quiet when she pulled up in front of Downeast Mortgage. There had been no explosion, no boom, everything was in place. Normal. Then the door flew open and Elsie Morehouse suddenly bolted down the steps, and it wasn't normal at all. Elsie was standing on the sidewalk, without a coat in ten-degree weather, screaming bloody murder, tears streaming down her face. Lucy grabbed the blanket she kept in the car in case of a breakdown and ran to Elsie, wrapping the blanket around her shoulders. Then she produced her phone and called the police department again.

"Tell them," she ordered, holding the phone.

"He's got a bomb," Elsie sobbed. "He says he's going to blow up Mr. Scribner."

"Move away from the building," Krissy ordered, in a calm, cool, and professional tone of voice. "I've got mutual aid on the way, the bomb squad, too. But the highway's closed due to the accident. . . . Move away from the building."

Lucy closed the phone and dragged Elsie down the street. Her gaze fell on the car, which she had left right in front of the Downeast building. No way, she thought, this isn't going to happen. There was no way she was going to lose her perfectly good but aged car, not when the insurance would only pay book value. Enough was enough, she thought, her blood rising. This had to stop.

She told Elsie to stay put and she ran back up the street to the Downeast building. At the door she paused for a moment, took a deep breath, then pulled it open. She stepped into the reception area where Ben Scribner was sitting behind Elsie's desk, tied to a chair, white as a sheet. Al Roberts was standing behind him, strapping his homemade bomb to Scribner's chest. "I don't want to do this, but you wouldn't get the message," he was saying. "I'd wear it myself, but I don't want my kidneys to get damaged."

"Good thinking," Lucy said, frantically scrolling through the directory on her phone, looking for Lexie's contact info.

"What the hell are you doing here?" Roberts demanded. His eyes were bright, and his chin had a couple of days' worth of stubble.

Lucy held up the phone. "I'm calling your daughter, Lexie, so you can say good-bye." Her fingers were shaking; she'd missed the directory key and the phone was telling her to reset her ring tones.

"Get out of here!" Roberts ordered. "I'm gonna blow this place to kingdom come, and don't think I won't." He paused, then added in a self-satisfied tone, "This bomb is just as big as the one I sent to Marlowe, and you know how that worked out."

Hearing this, Scribner grew even paler, and Lucy could see that his chin was quivering.

Roberts chuckled, a harsh, staccato sound. "You'd think this bastard here would get the idea, but nothing changed. The foreclosures didn't stop. Not even when his precious niece got hurt."

"What?' Scribner blinked, like a blind man who had suddenly recovered his sight. "What's this about Florence?"

"He rigged an accident—the stage scenery fell on her." Lucy couldn't master her voice, which quavered. "She's okay," she added.

"I didn't know," Scribner said.

"You don't know anything, that's the problem," Roberts said. "It's just business to you, not people's homes and lives."

Lucy took a deep breath. "I'm not going anywhere until you talk to Lexie," she said, hoping she sounded a lot braver than she felt. "This will ruin her life, you know."

Roberts was quick to reply. "I'm doing it for her, and Angie."

"You're doing it to get back at Scribner and Marlowe and everybody you think did you wrong," Lucy said. "Lexie will never forgive you."

"She'll get the insurance money."

"They won't pay for suicide," Lucy said, not sure if this was true or not.

"I checked. They will."

"What if the bomb doesn't kill you?" Lucy asked. "What if you survive and then you have to go to jail? There'll be no insurance then."

There was a sudden burst of noise from outside—a siren cut short. It was a mistake, a terrible mistake. The noise alerted Roberts that police had arrived and time was running out.

"You can trust me on this—there'll be no survivors," Roberts said. "Which is why you should get out of here. I'll give you five. . . ."

Scribner's eyes rolled up into his head and his chin dropped forward onto his chest.

"Hold on, what's the rush?" Lucy was backing toward the door.

"You called the cops," Scribner accused. "I'm not bluffing. Get out if you know what's good for you. Four." He paused a long moment, then said, "Three."

Roberts's eyes were glittering, and he was panting, hyperventilating. Lucy was utterly convinced he intended to blow himself, Scribner, and herself, too, into eternity. Heart pounding, Lucy turned and made a dash for the door when she was deafened by an enormously loud bang. Glass shattered. There was smoke and she couldn't breathe. She was coughing and her eyes were filled with tears. Her throat stung and she couldn't swallow. She collapsed, falling to the floor, discovering she was completely helpless and couldn't move. She thought of Bill, of the kids, and then she didn't think of anything at all.

*   *   *

When she came to, she was in an ambulance, and there was an oxygen mask over her face. A medic was leaning over her and she grabbed his arm.

"You're gonna be fine," he said. "Teargas. You had a reaction to the teargas."

"Bomb?" Her throat was raw and her voice came out as a croak.

"Didn't go off," he said. "The bomber's in custody. The other guy's fine—he refused treatment." He glanced up as the ambulance braked to a stop. "Well, here we are," he said, as she was wheeled into the emergency room. "Is there somebody you want me to call?"

Lucy shook her head. Not yet. She wasn't ready to explain to Bill, not yet. Even worse, what was she going to tell Rachel?

Chapter Twenty

It was truly ridiculous, Lucy thought, standing in the wings of the Community Church stage and waiting for her cue, but she felt more nervous about going onstage than she did when she charged into Downeast Mortgage that morning. Then Tiny Tim took his place in front of the toy shop window and she bustled onstage in her numerous petticoats and long, full skirt, carrying an enormous shopping basket. She was no longer Lucy Stone but instead was Mrs. Cratchit, fussing about whether nasty old Scrooge would allow her husband to spend Christmas Day with his family.

She was momentarily knocked out of character when her entrance was met with enthusiastic applause and even a few cheers. Word must have spread about her role in preventing the bombing, she realized as she waited for the audience to quiet down so she could deliver her line. She refused to think about that; in fact, she'd spent most of the day concentrating on not thinking about the entire episode.

"What were you thinking?" Bill had demanded, when she was released from the emergency room.

"I didn't think," Lucy had admitted, her voice a croak because her throat was still sore. "I didn't want the car to get blown up." She paused. "I know it was crazy."

"I'll say," Bill had muttered.

"I hope my voice comes back before tonight," she'd whispered. "I need to stop at the pharmacy and pick up some lozenges and throat spray."

She spent a quiet afternoon watching TV and sucking on lozenges and spraying her throat, and by supper time found her voice was almost normal. The phone rang quite a bit but she ignored it, telling herself she was saving her voice. The truth was she didn't want to talk about the confrontation with Al Roberts, didn't even want to think about it. Most of all, she didn't want to think about what was going to happen to Al, who would most probably spend the rest of his life in jail for sending the mail bomb that killed Jake Marlowe. So instead she flipped through old magazines and ate ice cream for lunch and searched the On Demand menu for old movies. Bill came home early and whipped up a creamy fettuccine Alfredo for dinner, but she didn't have much appetite, due to stage fright.

When she arrived at the church at the appointed time, Rachel greeted her with a hug. "I called and called. . . . I was afraid you couldn't go on tonight."

"Sorry," Lucy said. "I didn't answer the phone because I was saving my voice."

"You're forgiven." Rachel embraced her again. "Break a leg!"

Everyone in the cast was keyed up, and Lucy was afraid their nervousness would get in the way of their performances, but was pleased to discover it had the opposite effect. They were all on the top of their game and outdid themselves, and when Tiny Tim delivered the final line, "God bless us, everyone!" the hall erupted in cheers and stamping and clapping that went on for a very long time. The cast took one curtain call after another until they finally gave up and just stood there, clasping hands and basking in the outpouring of emotion. It was as if actors and audience were joined in one huge explosion of happy Christmas spirit.

Afterward, when Lucy had changed out of her costume, she was met at the dressing room door by Sara, who was holding an enormous bouquet of white carnations and red roses.

"For you, Mom," she said. "You were great."

This was the last thing Lucy expected, and she gave her daughter a big hug. "This is so sweet," she said, tears stinging her eyes. "Thank you."

"I haven't been very sweet lately and I'm sorry," Sara said.

Lucy's shoulders were shaking—she was crying her heart out. After holding herself together all day, she found she couldn't stop sobbing. Bill was there, holding her, and Rachel, too. Sara and Zoe were hugging each other, also crying.

"There, there, it's okay," Bill said, soothing her, and Lucy was trying to apologize for being so foolish, but couldn't seem to stop crying. Until finally, she did.

"You've had a tough day," Rachel said, wiping her own eyes and handing Lucy a wad of tissues.

"Let's go home," Bill urged.

"No," Lucy said, wiping her eyes.

"No?" Bill was surprised.

"I'm starving. Let's get a pizza."

"Great idea!" Bill agreed. "Let's go!"

* * *

On Monday morning, Lucy's spirits were still high when she went to work, buoyed by the equally successful performances on Saturday evening and Sunday afternoon. Everyone agreed that *A Christmas Carol* was the Community Players' best production in the group's twenty-year history. Lucy suspected that the group members may have had short memories, as it seemed to her that they always believed their last show was their best. Still, she was smiling when she pushed the door open and set the little bell to jangling.

"Shhh," Phyllis warned, pressing a raised finger to her lips.

"What's going on?" Lucy asked.

"Ted's meeting with Ben Scribner," she said, looking serious. "They've been in the morgue for at least half an hour."

"What's it about?" Lucy asked.

"I don't know, but Scribner was all business when he arrived, demanding an immediate meeting with Ted."

"You don't think he's calling the note, do you?" Lucy asked anxiously.

"That would take some nerve," Phyllis declared, "after what you did."

"Don't think I won't tell him that to his face," Lucy said, raising her voice.

At that moment the door to the morgue popped open and Lucy braced herself for bad news. Which, considering the fact that the two men were smiling and shaking hands, she immediately realized would not be necessary.

"This is excellent," Ted said. "I'm going to put my best reporter on it right away."

"On what?" Lucy asked, furrowing her brows.

"Ben here is developing a plan to sell back all the

foreclosed homes to their previous owners at the current, reduced value with new, affordable mortgages," Ted said. "He's also offering refinancing on favorable terms to all mortgagors, including me, who are struggling to keep up with payments due to the recession."

"What's the catch?" Phyllis asked, suspecting a trick.

"No catch!" declared Scribner, who for once looked relaxed and cheerful, actually seeming happy. "It's due to this lady here," he said, with a nod to Lucy. "She risked her life to save my miserable skin and it got me thinking. The truth is, Jake Marlowe and I got carried away. We got greedy. We didn't think about the people we were dealing with, and only thought about the money we were making. But when I was sitting there with that bomb strapped to my chest, I wasn't thinking about how much money I'd made. I was thinking that I'd wasted my life. And then you came, little lady, and gave me a second chance. Believe me, I've done some thinking and I'm not going to waste a single second of the time I've got left."

"That's . . . wonderful." Lucy was not quite sure what to say. It seemed to her that the earth had tilted on its axis and things were suddenly topsy-turvy.

"It's also good business," Scribner added, his blue eyes twinkling shrewdly. "What's the sense of a town where all the houses are empty and decaying? Truth is, I can't sell these properties. I've got too many on my hands and it's costing me money just to keep up with repairs and maintenance. Nope, this'll make our town, our community, stronger, and people will want to live in Tinker's Cove. Prices will start to go up again, and the sooner the better."

"It's too bad you didn't figure this out sooner," Phyllis said, adding a "hmph." "Coulda saved a lot of trouble."

Scribner's face clouded. "I know. I can't help but feel somewhat responsible for Al Roberts. I know there's no excuse for what he did, but Jake and I, well, we certainly contributed to his troubles. I'm going to make sure he gets a good lawyer, and I'm going to help his family any way I can, especially that little girl." He let out a big breath. "The truth is, I owe Roberts a huge debt. Jake Marlowe was a miserable person and now I'm free of him. I'm free to be myself and I'm determined to be a better person."

Hearing this admission, the three *Pennysaver* employees were dumbfounded. Finally, Ted spoke. "Is that for the record?"

"Hell, no!" Scribner said, his face reddening. "And don't think I won't sue!"

Then they were all laughing, laughing until their tummies hurt and they had to sit down, and finally they couldn't laugh anymore.

Word of Scribner's conversion spread through town as everyone was eager to share the story of his remarkable change of heart. Christmas spirit seemed to grow with every telling; people smiled and laughed and greeted each other cheerily as they hurried to complete their preparations for the big day. The people in line at the post office to mail cards and packages shared jokes and stories, people shopping for last minute presents waited patiently for the salesclerks to ring up their purchases, and shoppers at the IGA paused to chat with each other and exchange favorite holiday recipes. In Lucy's memory there had never been such a merry Christmas season in which everyone enjoyed such cheerful fellowship and genuine goodwill.

Lucy almost hated for it to end, but the number of remaining doors on the Advent calendar was down to two. And then there was only one and it was Christmas Eve. The presents were all bought and wrapped, the cookies baked, the tree decorated. The whole family went to church for the candlelight service; Patrick was adorable as a little lamb in the Christmas pageant. Afterward they all went on to Florence Gallagher's open house, bearing covered dishes for the potluck supper.

Florence's house was packed with people, but the jolly crowd was eager to make room for more. The table was loaded with delicious things to eat, carols were playing, everyone was eating and drinking and toasting the holiday. There was a hushed moment when Ben Scribner appeared, carrying a huge cooked turkey from MacDonalds' farm store, and Florence rushed to greet him with a big hug. Then others joined in the greeting, shaking hands and patting him on the back. Watching, Lucy thought he probably hadn't been greeted so warmly in many years, perhaps never.

She was chatting with Miss Tilley, telling her that the Angel Fund had swelled to over five thousand dollars thanks to a couple of large donations, including one from a secret giver she suspected was actually Ben Scribner, when she noticed Rachel and Bob, kissing under the mistletoe. She gave Miss Tilley a nudge, and the old woman smiled at the sight. "I've been so worried about Rachel," she said. "But now it looks like things are back on track."

"Moving in the right direction, anyway," Lucy said, taking a sip of eggnog.

A few minutes later Sue popped in, saying she couldn't stay long because she was on her way to New York. "Geoff's in surgery," she said. "He's getting a new kidney. He's part of a donation chain, which is actually the longest one they've done so far, with more than twenty exchanges. And guess what? Little Angie's getting a kidney, too! She's actually getting Sidra's kidney." She laughed. "My daughter's kidney is coming home to Tinker's Cove! Imagine!"

"It seems a toast is definitely called for," Miss Tilley said, tapping her glass with a spoon.

Everyone fell silent, waiting expectantly, as Miss Tilley called for all to "charge their glasses," using the old-fashioned phrase. When everyone's glass had been filled, she raised hers: "To friends and family, to Tinker's Cove . . . God bless us, everyone! Merry Christmas!"